I wondered why I assumed _____ _____ it all? Jodie, Leanne and Claire we.. __ __ __ bad, yet it was Lisa who bothered me. Instinctively I knew she was the ringleader. She had some kind of power – if I could identify what it was, maybe I would understand her better. She looked right, that was for sure. Her uniform was always untidy but her face was immaculate, even sophisticated. She wore foundation, blusher, lipstick and mascara. Everyone treated her as if she mattered, even the teachers, who either picked on her all the time, or side-stepped her, praising wherever they could. I thought that if Lisa approved of me, I'd be free to be myself and make my own friends. But clearly she didn't . . .

from The Women's Press

Sherry Ashworth lives in Manchester with her husband, two teenage daughters and two cats. She teaches English and Life Skills when she isn't writing novels, reviewing books, appearing on radio, or working as a freelance journalist. She enjoys reading, music, good friends, good food, and couldn't live without her computer.

What's Your Problem?

Sherry Ashworth

LiveWiRE

First published by Livewire Books, The Women's Press Ltd, 1999
A member of the Namara Group
34 Great Sutton Street, London EC1V 0LQ

British Library Cataloguing-in-Publication Data
A catalogue record for this book is available from the British Library.

ISBN 0 7043 4961 2

Typeset in Bembo 12/14pt by FSH Ltd, London
Printed and bound in Great Britain by Cox & Wyman Ltd, Reading,
Berkshire

To my daughters

Acknowledgements

With special thanks to Linda Kerr and Robyn Ashworth.

One

Last night I went back to the Lemon Tree for the first time. It wasn't my idea; my mates had decided that the Lemon Tree was the ideal place for our farewell party. To tell you the truth, I was pleased they'd suggested it. I was curious to see how I'd feel about the place now.

They do great coffee at the Lemon Tree, or so I was told by Rachel, who is passionate about cappuccino with a serious amount of cocoa powder on top. The Lemon Tree is an all-purpose arts centre in the middle of town, opposite the library. As you go in there's a café bar with loads of leaflets lying around on tables or pinned to display boards, advertising plays, concerts and poetry readings. The waiters are cute and have tiny blue aprons tied round their waists. Through the double doors at the back is the theatre. When I was younger there used to be a club night every month for sixteens and under, with techno music, soft drinks at the bar and bouncers standing around with their arms folded, looking fierce.

I went to one, once.

Tonight couldn't have been more different. My gang from college had colonised the table right by the window – Rachel, Jen, Shelly, Daniel, Mike and Louise. The minute I walked in Shelly shouted at me.

'Hi! Jac! We're over here!'

Not that anyone could have missed them. No one was as crazy as my mates. Shelly was wearing her hair in bunches, tied with pink ribbons. She was off to drama school. Jen's obsessed with body piercing, and she had all her gear on – earrings, nose stud and a new eyebrow ring. What she gets a kick out of is seeing people stare at her, and then telling them she's off to do a degree in theology. Louise, on the other hand, is going to be a nursery nurse, and the boys are taking a year out to try to make it in the music business. Rachel and I are also going to uni.

When I reached the table, I saw they'd saved a chair for me. Shelly stood up and air-kissed me on both cheeks, Ab-Fab style. It made me giggle.

'Can I get anyone a drink?' I asked, getting my purse from my bag.

'In a moment,' Shel said. 'But first we've got something for you.'

I was puzzled.

'Yeah. With your birthday being in November, and us all being in different places then, we decided to give you your pressie two months early.'

'Cool!' I'm afraid I'm a big kid when it comes to getting presents. I can't stand those people who always say

2

'you shouldn't have . . .' when they're faced with a gift. The truth is they can't wait to get their hands on it.

Shelly gave me an oblong parcel wrapped in blue metallic paper. Chocolates? A book? I opened it quickly, the paper crackling. It was a book, a writing book, with a bright yellow sun on the front.

'To remember us by,' Louise added. As if I could ever forget them!

I began to turn the pages. Inside were photographs of all of my friends, some in daft poses. On some pages they'd written messages, old jokes we'd shared, and pleas to come and stay with me at uni. There were ticket stubs from nights out together and the programme from the play we were all in at our sixth-form college. Mike had written a poem and Shelly had drawn a cartoon of me, labelling it to show all my quirks.

As I continued to turn the pages, my hands were trembling. Nothing they could have chosen would have meant so much to me. I'm not the crying sort, but the backs of my eyes were pricking and the hug that Rachel gave me finished me off. It was enough to make my mascara run – a fact that Dan kindly pointed out as soon as I'd broken away from Rachel.

'Has anyone got a mirror?' No one had. 'I'll just pop to the loo and tidy up, then.'

It was a relief to have a moment to myself, because I was feeling rather emotional. It was a combination of knowing I was leaving home in a week and saying goodbye to my friends. This present was the last straw. Luckily the loos were empty, so I was able to take a paper towel and blow my nose loudly, then dampen my finger and dab at my streaked mascara. My fault, I suppose, for wearing so much make-up, but I love it, and when I get stressed out I'm either down at the cosmetics counter at Boots, or experimenting with my selection of shadows at home. Just now I like the sixties look, with loads of thick eyeliner. I wear my hair straight and long. I have a centre parting and I still have a fringe, though I can't decide whether to grow it out or not. I looked at myself for a moment longer, wondering whether to reapply my lipstick, and then thinking that I'd be having a drink soon, so it didn't matter. I began to fiddle with my hair, making it fall just right. It was something I did automatically, a sort of nervous habit. It was something I'd done for years.

I think now it was that gesture that did it; the way I pulled my hair forward ever so slightly. I suddenly connected with the person that was here three years ago, a different Jac. I was growing out my hair then from a short style and was still coping with the remains of teenage zits. The concealer I'd put on was blotchy in places, and my eyes, when I'd looked in the mirror at myself, had been childlike; wide and scared. For a moment I could almost taste my fear. Again I knew what it was like to stand here utterly alone, no friends outside, no friends at all.

I shivered and gently brought myself back to the present. They were the bad old days but I knew I would never be able to forget them. They had changed me for ever. When, I wondered, had it all begun? Certainly not that night at the Lemon Tree, not even when I first started at Markfield. It started, you could say, the night I overheard Dad saying we would have to move house.

Two

I was in my room, finishing off some homework with the radio turned down low. I wasn't really concentrating on my geography because I was half-listening for the phone to ring, as Rachel said she would call if she was able to sleep over. I didn't hear the phone, but I caught the sound of my parents talking. I stopped what I was doing so I could concentrate and try to make out what they were saying. Eavesdropping is my speciality. You wouldn't believe the things you can find out. This time, what intrigued me was the tone of their voices, determined, important sounding. I kicked my door wide open to catch what they were saying.

'You see these figures? I think we could free around twenty thousand of capital, even after allowing for estate agents' fees and the solicitors' bills.'

'Twenty thousand! That's more than enough to start you off.'

'And it gives us a little bit left over to play with. I might need to trade the car in for a Transit.'

'I suppose we could manage in a smaller house. There'd be less housework, for a start.'

'It would only be temporary, Sheila.'

'Perhaps we'll get to like it.'

I frowned to myself. A smaller house? Who would be living in a smaller house? Us? Even though my dad was temporarily out of work, he'd always put on a brave face to me, and made out that everything would soon be on a firmer footing. I didn't know that moving house was on the cards. I didn't know how I felt about that. I'd lived in Bank View all my life – it *was* my life. I turned off my radio and strained to hear more, but now my parents were speaking with lowered voices.

Moving house. It might not be such a bad idea. Our house was quite old and too large for the three of us. The high ceilings made it look a bit old-fashioned compared to some of my friends' houses. I liked my room, but I was always on at my parents to get it redecorated – even though I had tons of posters up, it still looked a bit tatty. What I really wanted was a modern bedroom, done out in bright, jazzy colours, a wardrobe with loads of room for clothes and a good music system of my own or even just a cheap stereo. A TV might be pushing it a bit too far...

Come to think of it, moving house could be quite exciting. I hadn't understood all of what my parents were saying, but I had taken note of the tone of their voices. They sounded cheerful again; I'd begun to think they couldn't do cheerful any more, not since the day Dad lost his job. If moving house would give us all a fresh start, it was certainly worth considering. Perhaps I would even be allowed to have a say in where we went. We could move nearer to Rachel's. I pushed my geography to one side and went to join my parents.

They were in Dad's study. Don't get the wrong idea about this – his study wasn't one of those book-lined mahogany affairs. It was just the box room, and all it had in it was his computer workstation, piles of box files and a couple of rickety old chairs. Mum was sitting on one, and Dad was in front of the computer screen.

'Are we going to move house, then?' I said to them.

My mother looked at me apprehensively. 'Were you listening?'

'Might have been.' I grinned at them. 'I think it's a great idea. I'd like to move.'

My parents exchanged a meaningful look. They were always doing that. What they didn't realise was that I was an expert in decoding them. There was Shall We Let Her?; You Tell Her, I Can't; and Only If You Think So, Dear. This time they both looked nervous, as if I'd caught them with their hands in the cookie jar. Was there something else, something I hadn't heard?

'I said, I don't mind moving.'

My father rubbed his chin thoughtfully, stole a glance at my mother, attempted to look at me, then began to study a spot on his desk. Then, summoning his resolve, he looked at me directly.

'I think you're old enough to be put in the picture. Since I've been out of work, we've had to find ways of saving money. We've already had to dip into our savings, which isn't something we've liked doing. There isn't the prospect of a job on the horizon except' – he paused – 'except if I were to start up a business of my own. Do you know what a franchise is?'

I didn't. This was beginning to sound more like an economics lesson than a family chat.

'I buy a share in an established business and then I own and manage the branch. There's the possibility of a franchise from Carpets Direct. It looks interesting, and I'd like to go ahead. But we'll need a large sum of money to buy the franchise. That's why we need to sell the house.'

Blah, blah, blah . . . There are some disadvantages to being treated as an adult.

'And also it will be some time before we show a profit. Mum's money will be helpful – vital, in fact – but as you know, she only works part-time, and she isn't able to increase her hours. We need to make other economies, too.'

I said a mental goodbye to my new stereo.

'We had an idea,' my father said. 'We wouldn't mention it, but you've been complaining quite a lot recently about school.'

This was true. When I was eleven my parents had insisted I sit the entrance exam for Chillingham, a private girls-only school. When I was younger it was all right, but recently all the petty uniform restrictions and nagging teachers scaring you senseless about the GCSEs had been driving me and Rach demented. We knew the exams were important. Why did they have to keep on telling us?

'The fees at Chillingham eat up a lot of our income.'

Now I was listening more carefully. Something was up.

'Just let me run this past you.'

He was talking in business jargon. What was he trying to hide?

'What if you moved schools, and took your GCSEs at Markfield?'

Moved schools?

'I've heard some very good things about Markfield,' my mother intervened. 'They were top of the league table last year and compared very well with Chillingham. Not that one is supposed to set much store by league tables. I've made a few enquiries, and they use the same examination board as Chillingham so you'd be following the same syllabuses. The change might be very stimulating for you.'

I'll tell you what got me – not so much the idea of changing schools, but the fact that my mother had begun making enquiries without even consulting me. Just a few moments ago I was old enough to be put in the picture, and now they were treating me like a kid! They think they can have it both ways, just as it suits them. But my school is my own business and Mum had no right to find out stuff without telling me what she was up to. Sometimes they both still behave as if my life was their life. My expression was stony and I said nothing.

'Jac, don't sulk,' my mother pleaded.

She always said I was sulking when I wasn't. I was trying to come to terms with what they had just said. Part of me thought it was probably a joke, and in a moment they'd start laughing, and reality would resume. But they didn't laugh. Leave Chillingham. That meant leaving Rachel, and she was my best friend. Chillingham wasn't a perfect school in many respects, but it was my school and I knew it. It was familiar. There was a hollow pit of despair in my stomach.

'We wouldn't suggest it,' my father said, 'if we didn't

think you'd benefit in the long run. When we sent you to Chillingham originally the state schools in the area were reorganising, and everything was in chaos. But Markfield has made a name for itself now. It would only be for one year, and then you could apply for the sixth-form college.'

'Look, isn't there another way you could save money? Can't we make economies with clothes, or food or something?'

'We couldn't save as much. And they've hiked the fees up for the next year, *and* you'll need a new uniform.'

'I'm sorry I cost you so much money!' I tried to sound as sarcastic as I possibly could. I glanced at my mother, who looked stricken. I could see I had hurt her.

'Jac!' my father said warningly.

'Forget it.' I stormed out of the study, slamming the door as loudly as I could. I knew I would be in trouble later but I didn't care. I just wanted them to know how much they'd upset me. But looking back I can see there was more to it. I felt powerless. I couldn't understand why at fifteen I was actually scared of going to another school, and I didn't want to admit that either to myself or to my parents. What if I didn't fit in? What if no one liked me?

I ran into my bedroom and threw myself on my bed, breathing hard and fighting back the tears. My parents were so selfish! I couldn't possibly leave Chillingham. I thought they loved me, and now it seemed I was just a set of figures on Dad's computer – we can save money on Jac's education! I felt betrayed and wondered about running away or doing something to make them regret what they'd just suggested. Running away might work. I imagined them frantic, phoning the police, Mum saying to Dad how it was her fault, and Dad saying to Mum that it was his fault, and both of them resolving never to utter another harsh word to me. As I thought this, I realised how babyish that reaction was. I also realised that my last remark to them was nasty and calculated. I didn't feel too good about it now.

When I heard Mum's footsteps approaching I stiffened. She entered my bedroom and I turned my face to the wall. She came and sat down on the edge of the bed and began to stroke my hair, pushing it away from my face as she's always done. I did not react.

'If you really want to stay at Chillingham, we'll let you. We would never force you to go.'

Now I felt awful. My mother continued playing with my hair and, mixed with the relief, I felt a nagging disappointment. Chillingham could be a pain at times – teachers telling you to straighten your skirt, and all the kids from other schools calling you a snob. True, I'd miss Rachel, but there wasn't anyone else I cared for that much. I was old enough to know that how well I did in my GCSEs depended mostly on how hard I worked, not on the teachers. I knew a little about Markfield, and just recently they'd opened up a brand-new drama studio. I loved acting, and that appealed to me. Also there was the question of boys.

Chillingham was an all-girls school. It was a big disadvantage, particularly for me and Rach, because neither of us had brothers. Brothers are one way of getting to know boys, and that was closed to us. There was a youth club we used to go to, but the leader left and no one took her place. Even that was mostly girls, and the boys who went ignored us. Last term a girl at school set us up with some friends of her boyfriend, but Rachel was so shy she didn't utter a word all evening, and I spoke for the two of us because I was so nervous. They didn't ask us out again and we didn't ask them either. We didn't see the point in going out with boys just for the sake of it – that was so sad. We wanted something real, something worthwhile. But how on earth were we going to meet *anyone*?

There would be boys at Markfield. Hordes of them. There were no petty uniform restrictions, and I imagined that the atmosphere would be more relaxed than at Chillingham, where the teachers were in the habit of counting the days to your GCSEs.

'I didn't say I wouldn't go to Markfield,' I said to my mother.

She stopped stroking my hair.

'It was just a shock,' I continued. 'I'd like to think about it.'

'There's no pressure on you.'

'If I did go to Markfield, would we be able to have a holiday this summer?'

'Well, I . . . It might do us good. I suppose we could rent a cottage somewhere.'

'On the coast. And we could take Rachel.'

My mother laughed, and I detected some relief in her laugh. I think it was then that I made up my mind to go to Markfield. There was something so tempting about making everyone happy. When you think about it, school is only from nine to four, but you have to live with your family all the time. My parents aren't the easiest people – whose are? My mother is the worrying, overprotective

12

type, and my father gets moods, and both of them only treat me as a grown-up when it suits them. On the other hand, we could have fun too, and we hadn't had any fun for a while. If my leaving Chillingham would help us all lighten up, it would be worth it.

Three

The sky was cobalt blue and the sun beat down on our bodies. Well, mostly on my body, as Rachel was wearing a T-shirt over her swimsuit and a cheesecloth sarong over her legs. She said she was scared of getting sunburnt, but I knew she was a bit self-conscious about her weight. Not that she had any reason to be – she was a gorgeous blond with a smile that made you smile, too. I had my bikini on, plus loads of tanning lotion.

Mum had insisted on joining us, and she had fallen asleep in her deckchair, her novel on the towel by her side. It was fat and swollen with all the sand that had sneaked into the corners of the pages. Dad had gone off for a walk somewhere – even in the heat he has to be on the move. Rach and I had been trying to get lads to notice us. You know the sort of thing, laughing and smiling whenever anything decent walked by. Now she was lying face-up and I couldn't tell whether she was asleep or not because she had sunglasses on. They were great shades, with thick pink frames like a movie star's. I sat up, suddenly bored with lying down and doing nothing. I was feeling restless. I stared out to sea. It was dotted with children in bright costumes and their distant cries sounded like birds calling. Further out the sea looked mottled, squares of darker blue mingling with flecks of pale turquoise. In the far distance was the horizon. I idly wondered where I would get to if I started walking towards it and just carried on going.

Rachel's voice broke my reverie. 'What are you thinking about, Jac?'

'Nothing.'

'You can't be thinking about nothing. It's impossible to empty your mind completely.'

'I disagree.'

'Go on. Try it.'

'Bet you I can.'

'Bet you you can't.'

I assumed a half-lotus position, crossed my arms and tried to look as if I was thinking about nothing. Of course Rachel was right. I was thinking about thinking about nothing, and then I noticed the warmth of the sun on my back, and felt the grittiness of the sand on my calves.

'There we are. I'm thinking about nothing,' I said.

'As if,' she said.

'D'you fancy a 99?' I suggested.

'You're on.'

We woke up Mum and offered to get her one too.

As we walked to the promenade, Rachel said to me, 'I'll miss you.'

'What do you mean, miss me?'

'When you go to Markfield.'

'No, you won't. We'll still see each other loads, only not at school.'

'I'll have no one to go round with.'

'There's Payel and Lauren.'

'I know.' Rachel's voice was wistful. 'But hey, here I am whinging about me, and it's you who's starting a new school next week. Do you feel all right about it?'

'Kind of. I am nervous, but I suppose anyone would be. Can you imagine what a prat I'd look if I got lost on the first day, and me a fifth year?'

Rachel laughed as she sidestepped a sandcastle topped with a little yellow flag with a red lion on it. 'Is that all you're nervous about?'

'Well, no – it's the whole business of settling in, feeling new and everything. I hope I make friends quickly.'

'You will make friends,' she said, 'only it will probably take a little time. You can always talk to the teachers if there are problems. And don't beat yourself up if you feel shy. Everyone feels shy in the beginning.'

'Have you ever thought of a career as an agony aunt?' I ribbed her. 'Try solving this one. *My best mate Rachel is boy-crazy – she can't keep her eyes off them. It's driving me mad and –* '

'Shut up, you!' She picked up a handful of sand and flung it at me.

'Right! I'm getting you for that.' I picked up two handfuls. She began to run away from me and I pursued

16

her, although we were both laughing so much we could hardly run.

I didn't have a care in the world then. Little did I know it was the last time I'd feel completely happy for a long, long while.

Four

Suddenly I was awake. There was sunlight streaming through my windows, casting unfamiliar shadows in my room. My radio alarm hadn't come on yet and for a moment I thought I hadn't set it properly and had overslept. I would be late for school on my first day. Great. I wriggled out of the duvet and sat up. It was only 6.38.

My wardrobe was open, and I could see my Markfield uniform hanging on the small rail attached to the door. White shirt, dark blue tie with a pale blue stripe, navy skirt. Seeing it there, limp and lifeless, made me nervous. They were only clothes, but once I put them on I would be a new me, a different person. I sat cross-legged under my duvet and thought for a while. I knew I had a habit of overdramatising things, and I talked to myself sensibly for a bit.

New beginnings were nothing to be afraid of. For

example, the day we'd moved to this house had turned out fine. Of course the removal van was late and Mum panicked, thinking they'd got the wrong day, but Dad was in a good mood and everything went like clockwork after that. Since the kitchen wasn't straight by the evening, we decided to get a Chinese takeaway. Dad and I drove round the neighbourhood until we found the Kowloon, which was conveniently just next door to Victoria Wine. Before too long we were all camping out in front of the TV, eating sweet and sour chicken and prawn crackers, washed down with sparkling white wine.

Our new house was small, but modern, and my room was at the back. It overlooked our garden as well as everybody else's. When I should have been unpacking and hanging up clothes I knelt on my bed and looked out of the window at an old man gardening, cats staring each other out on garage roofs and a woman hanging out washing. Gradually in the next weeks I found my way around and even discovered a local library three streets away. I've always been a sucker for a good book – it's the way you can get right inside how somebody else thinks and feels. That's why I like acting, too. It's interesting, pretending to be other people.

So I was quite happy in the new house. I reckon Mum missed the old place a bit, but she was the only one. If moving school was as bad as moving house, I had nothing to worry about. As soon as I had made some friends I knew I would be fine. With a burst of optimism I sprang out of bed and made for the bathroom.

I wore my backpack on one shoulder and made my way towards Markfield High. Ahead of me people walked in twos and threes, except for kids who were obviously first years in uniforms that were at least two sizes too big for them. It made me smile to think that in a way I was a new kid too, only starting in year 11. I had an advantage over them, being older, but in a way I guess I was as nervous as they were.

Markfield was at the end of the road, a square, old-fashioned, redbrick building with a tarmac playground in front of it. I knew that behind this sprawled a maze of annexes and corridors and extensions that I would have to find my way around. For now I headed straight to the main entrance. I pushed open the door and found myself in a modern reception area, with a woman sitting at a desk with a computer station, and several other adults standing around. I went up to the desk.

'Excuse me. I'm new here. I was told to ask for the head of year 11, Mrs Thornton.'

The woman at the desk looked pointedly at one of the other people who I guessed were probably teachers. The youngest one, a man, told me to follow him. I set off down a corridor smelling of fresh paint, walking a pace or two behind. I could hear shouts from inside classrooms and felt the buzz of a place filling with people. Now I was actually in Markfield my fear was changing into excitement.

We reached a door painted red and the teacher vanished. In a few moments another teacher appeared, who was very obviously pregnant.

'I'm Mrs Thornton, head of year 11. And you must be Jacintha Elliot.'

Her voice was warm and friendly, but I had to put her right on one thing.

'Everyone calls me Jac,' I said. 'I can't stand my name. It's after an aunt of my mother's. It was her dying wish that her name should live on.'

Mrs Thornton laughed. 'But Jac is nice. It suits you. Come on, then. We'll pop into my office and then I'll take you to your new class. It's one of the English rooms.'

That felt like a good omen. English was my favourite subject. Feeling a little more cheerful, I followed Mrs Thornton down the corridor. She ushered me into her office, a tiny room with a window giving out on to a small yard with some builders' equipment in it.

'There are a few forms I'd like you to fill in,' she began, easing herself into her chair.

'I'm rubbish at filling in forms,' I said. 'I always put my surname where my first name should go, and things like that.'

I could hear myself babbling. I knew it was a sign I was nervous. I tried to concentrate on the forms but I could feel myself going again. 'When are you expecting your baby?' I asked her.

'In a couple of months,' she replied.

'Is it your first? My mum only had me – apparently I was so much trouble, crying all night and she was sick all through the pregnancy – it put her off.'

I was wittering again. When I was little and my mum took me to the dentist, he couldn't even manage to give me an examination because I wouldn't shut up. I suppose talking made me feel in control of what was going on – or stopped me thinking. I told Mrs Thornton about our move, and how I enjoyed acting, and how funny it was to see Dad humping carpets about, and how he nearly put his back out. I was pleased when she smiled. Eventually she hoisted herself off the chair, we left her office, and I guessed I was on my way to my new class.

Now the school was busier than ever and it did seem odd to have so many boys around. Most of them seemed smaller than me. The English department was up a flight of stairs and along a passageway that had a view of a back playground where there were picnic tables. Finally we came to some classrooms, and Mrs Thornton opened one of the doors.

There was no teacher there but about fifteen people, some boys, some girls.

'This is Jac Elliot,' Mrs Thornton said. 'She's new to Markfield. Anyone going to volunteer to look after her?'

I wished she hadn't said that. It was as bad as when the games teacher asks someone to choose teams and you're left till last. I felt as conspicuous as a Christmas tree in midsummer.

'We'll look after her, Miss,' came a voice.

I filled with relief and smiled at the girl who had spoken. She was about my height, quite thin, with light brown hair and a thick fringe. Mrs Thornton disappeared, leaving me feeling like an alien who'd just landed in front of a crowd of mystified locals.

'I'm Leanne,' said the girl with light brown hair. 'This is Jodie.' Jodie was standing next to her, a short girl with dyed black hair. She grinned at me, and that made me feel loads better. I was still nervous, but mixed with my nervousness was a feeling of anticipation. We might all turn out to be really close friends. Who could say?

'I'm Jac,' I said again.

'That's a boy's name,' Leanne commented.

'No – mine is spelt J-a-c. It's an abbreviation. It's like

22

being called Sam or Jo.'

My voice seemed to echo round the classroom. I immediately regretted my explanation. Why couldn't I just shut up and let other people do the talking?

'Do you live round here?' Leanne asked.

'Yes. In the estate at Canning Hill Park. We moved there a few weeks ago.'

'I know Canning Hill Park,' Jodie said, making me feel I'd given the right answer. I was fitting in. I was doing OK. I began to relax.

'So where did you go to school before?'

'Chillingham,' I blurted out. I could have kicked myself.

'That's a snob school, isn't it?'

'No, it isn't... I know it's got a bit of a reputation but we're dead normal when you get to know us... Honest. The school isn't much different from Markfield, except for the boys.'

I blushed even more. Now Leanne and Jodie would think I'd never spoken to boys before.

'Why d'you leave Chillingham?'

'Because we moved.'

'But Canning Hill Park is quite near Chillingham.'

I was getting flustered. I didn't want to explain about Dad losing his job, but to be honest I think I would have done, and told them the whole story of why I ended up at Markfield – I could feel a confession fit coming on – but thankfully I was stopped by the arrival of another girl.

'Is Lisa here yet?'

'No. I saw her last night, though. She finished with Damon.'

'You're kidding!'

23

'No way. She said he was getting too clingy, hanging round her all the time. She wanted him off her back.'

They had obviously forgotten about me. I stood there, my school bag still over my shoulder, listening to their gossip and feeling a little out of it. It gave me time to survey the classroom. There were some boys at the back who weren't looking our way. There were dog-eared posters advertising last year's production of *Macbeth* at the Lemon Tree and a section of wall where the paint was peeling. All of a sudden I was swept with a desire to be back at Chillingham. Only now there was no going back. Then I heard my name mentioned.

'This is Jac,' Jodie said. 'She's new.'

The new arrival gave me the once over. 'I'm Claire,' she said. 'Hi.'

'Hi,' I said. I wanted to say something nice to her. 'Hey, I like your shoes!' She was wearing huge platforms.

'Yeah. They're from Shoe Express.'

Then Claire looked towards the door, and one by one we all did the same. Our teacher had come in. He was about my father's age, tallish, and with a stomach that stuck out over his trousers. He was wearing a suit that looked rather creased.

'Oh no, it's you lot!' he said.

There were some groans from the class. We had sarcastic teachers like that at Chillingham, too. You normally play along with them, but they make you feel uncomfortable. The teacher put his briefcase on the desk and began to take out registers and papers. People drifted to their seats. The desks were arranged in twos. Leanne and Jodie sat down together, Claire went to sit behind them and I decided to sit next to her. She had seemed quite friendly.

24

'What's his name?' I asked her.

'Mr Weston.'

'Is he OK?'

''S all right. He shouts a lot.'

As if to cue, he raised his voice.

'RIGHT. I've got your timetables here and you'd better listen because if you don't and you end up in the physics lab when you've got cookery it's going to be your own fault. You can each take one of these masters – '

He stopped in his tracks. The door opened, squeaking as it did so. There was a latecomer. In came a girl, nearly as tall as me, her blouse hanging loose over a skirt that was defiantly short. Her backpack swung from one shoulder.

'Bus was late, sir,' she explained casually, as if she were his equal. She looked around the classroom, saw me and frowned. She walked over.

'You're sitting in my place,' she said.

'I'm sorry.'

I quickly gathered my things and moved away. There was an empty double desk at the front and I took a seat there. I was conscious that I was blushing, of a flurry of whispered conversation, then Mr Weston's booming voice telling everyone to shut up.

'Lisa Webb. We'll start as we mean to go on. If you're late again tomorrow, it's a detention.'

I couldn't resist turning round to steal a glance at her. Her face was utterly blank, as if she hadn't heard him. Her expression wasn't exactly insolent, but in the absence of acknowledgement there was a challenge to him. I thought she was rather scary. Then she took a lipgloss from her pocket and began to apply it. Mr Weston just

25

went back to dishing out the timetables. I made myself try to pay attention – I didn't want to get lost on the first day. Only it was hard – I felt vaguely uneasy and my mind kept going back to the two conversations I'd just had. I regretted saying I'd come from Chillingham and sitting in Lisa's seat. Why didn't they tell me it belonged to her? I'd felt so foolish having to gather up all my stuff and move like that in front of the whole class.

At Chillingham, because I knew everyone, it was easy to keep out of trouble. Here, I realised, I was as green as they come. I felt a bit scared, and lonely too. There was no Rachel, no one, in fact, who would take me on one side and explain the unwritten rules. For a moment I was tempted to get up and just walk out but I told myself to snap out of it and began to try and make sense of the timetable. The morning passed in a blur.

I wasn't alone with my class again until lunchtime. At break, Mr Weston had taken me to stationery, and then there had been a year assembly. Now we were left to disperse. I had some sandwiches in my bag that Mum had made, but I wasn't sure where to eat them. Among other things, Mr Weston had given me a form for my parents to sign giving me permission to go out at lunchtime. I was trying to decide what to do when I saw Leanne, Jodie, Claire and Lisa approaching. I tensed, hoping Lisa had forgiven me for taking her seat.

'What're you doing for lunch?'

'I don't know. I've got some sandwiches.'

'We're going down the chippy. D'you want to come?'

'Oh, all right.' I hoped I hadn't sounded too non-committal, or too eager. It was impossible to know how

26

to act. I felt as if I was balancing on a tightrope.

Then Jodie smiled at me, which made me feel better. I followed them out of school, thinking that they were quite friendly, possibly even friendlier to me than we would have been to a newcomer at Chillingham. I looked forward to sharing that thought with Rachel.

There was a parade of shops five minutes' walk away. We passed a post office, a butcher's with a model of a butcher with a stripy apron and a tray of meat outside, a newsagent's, a chemist's and finally the fish and chip shop. Already there was a queue of people from Markfield. I felt glad that I was having my lunch in the right place – obviously only first years and saddos hung out in the canteen.

Everyone seemed to know Lisa, especially the boys. They were making remarks to her, and she was insulting them. Maybe that was how you did it, I thought. Maybe Rachel and I were just too nice. She was treating the boys as if they were dirt and they seemed to be lapping it up. Her voice was bored and sardonic. Standing on the outside watching all of this made me feel a bit of a spare part again.

Eventually Lisa rejoined us in the queue and began to tidy her hair. It was fair but with a reddish, strawberry tint to it. She wore it up with a butterfly clip at the back, but she let two tendrils escape on either side to frame her face. Her complexion was so even I was sure she was wearing foundation. I think if I'd seen her out of school I'd have thought she was a lot older than me. She seemed sophisticated, and sophisticated was the last thing I felt right then. Because I was growing my hair out it had reached that messy stage when you can't do a thing with it and you're thinking of getting it cut again. In the wind it was blowing everywhere. My uniform looked brand new – which it was – and everyone else's was fashionably tatty. I wasn't wearing much make-up and knew I had zits on my forehead. Rather than look at the boys, I looked into the interior of the chippy.

Just the sight of the food made me realise I was starving. As we edged inside I could smell the delicious aroma of frying food, and saw under the glass counter a row of pies and a line of golden, battered fish, warm and crisp. Everyone was ordering chips, so I did, and I got a cherry Coke to go with them. The chips were served up in a cone with a little plastic fork. I followed the girls outside and we began to eat as we walked back to school. They were talking about people they knew and I was content just to listen, to eat and be accepted.

Lisa led us to the area of the playground where I'd seen some picnic tables. We settled into an empty one, tucking ourselves between the fixed seats and the table. It reminded me of when we had stopped on our way to our cottage in the summer.

'This is almost like being on holiday,' I said, immediately regretting my daft comment as soon as I'd said it. Lisa gave me a peculiar look.

'You must have funny holidays,' she said.

I tried to explain what I meant. 'It's just the picnic table,' I said lamely. 'At my old school we were only allowed to eat in the canteen. And picnic tables remind me of going on holiday. We went to Southpool this year. Me and my mate Rachel.' I was doing it again, wittering on pointlessly.

'D'you pull anyone?' Lisa asked.

'Nearly,' I bluffed.

'Nearly?'

The other girls giggled. I felt hot and embarrassed and out of my depth. I hated myself for my stupid answer. I tried to cover up, stammering badly.

'We would have, but, like – you know – my parents – they were a pain...'

My excuse sounded even worse than my gaffe. I was drowning. Somebody help me! Lisa and Leanne and Jodie and Claire just watched me plunge. I tried to change the subject.

'Did you go away?' I asked Lisa.

'Yeah, Miami,' she said, her face neutral. She glanced at Claire, who sniggered.

'That must have been nice,' I ventured.

Now all the girls laughed and I realised Lisa had been having me on.

'Sorry,' I said, 'I thought you were being serious. I'd love to go to Miami, but there's no chance of that for a bit – my dad lost his job, and now he's just started up his own business, selling carpets. My mum's a teacher – she teaches English, but at a college of higher education. I'd hate to be a teacher – I'd like to act one day. Imagine being on one of the soaps! I was in a few plays at my old school. We did the *Wizard of Oz* and I was a...'

I couldn't believe I was doing this – wittering on again, and I was about to confess I had been a Munchkin! That would certainly send my street cred shooting up. Only something was compelling me to talk, to fill up the void that my initial comments had created. The thing is, I seemed to be making matters worse. They all looked as if they found me faintly amusing.

'Somebody stop me,' I said. 'I go on and on sometimes. Sorry.'

Now I know it wasn't so much the fact I sounded a fool, as that one word 'sorry'. It opened me up, and showed them how vulnerable I felt. After all, I had nothing to apologise for. But at the time I was so desperate to fit in, to get some acknowledgement that they liked me, that I would have done anything. I never stopped to ask myself if I actually liked them. What they thought of me meant everything. They were the critics; I was on-stage – an actor without a script, making up my lines as I went along, and I had a sinking feeling that I was getting them all wrong.

'What time's afternoon registration?' I asked in a small voice.

'If you want to be *early*,' Lisa said, emphasising the last word, 'you'd better go now.'

I had the distinct impression they wanted me to go. To be honest, I was glad to be going. I took my rubbish to put in a bin and picked up my backpack.

'Bye!' I said, as nonchalantly as I could.

I made my way back to school, walking quickly in my nervousness. Any further thoughts on the subject of Lisa came to an abrupt halt. As I entered the main building I found myself outside the new drama studio. The doors leading to it were shut, but pinned to one of them there was a notice that caught my eye.

AUDITIONS FOR 'AN INSPECTOR CALLS'
ON THURSDAY LUNCHTIME. YEARS 10 AND 11.
Just turn up or see Mr Jennings.

I couldn't believe my luck. They were putting on a play, and it was one I'd studied at Chillingham. It was about a girl – Eva Smith – who'd committed suicide and would own up to their responsibility for her death – except Sheila Birling. That'd be the part I'd like, I thought. I forgot about my awkward lunch with Lisa and her friends. I hoped that by taking part in a cast of a play, I'd make other friends who'd like me more. Besides, I loved acting. It was a chance to be another person, to shed the old Jac and become someone totally different. I knew Mum had a copy of the play at home, and I decided to practise reading from it that night, so I could wow them at the auditions. After I'd rung Rachel, of course.

'Jac! It's me, Rach. How did you get on?'

'OK. Well, you know. It was a bit terrifying at times, being the new girl.'

'Poor you. D'you make any friends?'

'Well, not exactly. I haven't found anyone quite my type yet. I did have lunch with some girls, though.'

'Were they all right?'

'Yeah, sort of. But listen – they're going to put on *An Inspector Calls*. They're going to have auditions.'

'How cool is that? You'd make a brilliant Sheila Birling.'

'Yes, but I might not get the part. I don't know who else will turn up to auditions.'

'You must have a go.'

'Of course I will. Oh, Rach, I miss you. How was Chillingham?'

'Gross. It's like prison. But there's a new hockey teacher; she was in a national squad . . .'

'Jac? How long have we been on the phone for?'

'I don't know. You rang me after *EastEnders*.'

'Omigod! It's quarter to ten! And Dad's coming down the stairs. He'll *kill* me.'

'I'll go. Speak to you tomorrow.'

We exchanged goodbyes and I put the receiver down. Rachel and I try to hide from our dads how much we're on the phone. Why is it fathers never understand how important it is just to talk? Especially tonight. I'd enjoyed listening to Rachel go on about school, and I could almost imagine I was back there. I'd said very little to her about Markfield, and particularly the horrible lunch I'd had. I guess I was trying to block it out. I just wanted to pretend none of it had happened, to erase the whole scene. For all I knew, Lisa could come in tomorrow and be perfectly friendly. It could happen. Who's to say it wouldn't? Why worry before you have to?

'Have you been on the phone all that time?' my father said, poking his head out from behind the living-room door.

'Rachel called me!' I shot at him.

He harrumphed at me, foiled. I smiled at having got the upper hand and decided to relax and watch a little more telly before I made my way to bed.

Five

When I arrived at the drama studio there were already a few people waiting. They were sitting on the front row facing the stage. Behind them rose tiers of plastic seats in alternate red and grey. The stage was in darkness but the house lights were on and I was able to scan the people there to see if I recognised anyone, as unlikely as that was.

They were all strangers. I put my backpack down at the end of the row and sat on a chair next to it, hoping someone would come up to me. I attracted a few curious glances, none hostile, but none particularly friendly either. Rachel was right; it was going to take time to make new friends. Some of the girls in my class were talking to me, but only now and then. It made me feel as if I was there on probation.

The door opened, and three boys walked in. I didn't recognise them either but looked at them much longer than

I should have done. You wouldn't have blamed me. All three of them were totally fit. One of them was short with a lovely, infectious smile; there was another decidedly cute boy with a baby face and an Adidas bag, and another with strikingly dark hair and a serious face. He was the one I couldn't take my eyes off. It almost felt like I recognised him from somewhere, but of course I'd never seen him before in my life. Because there were some empty seats close to me they came and sat by me, and the dark-haired boy said hi.

'Hi,' I said, my heart thumping.

Then a teacher came out from the wings – the same teacher who'd taken me to the staff room on my first day. I smiled at him, hoping he'd recognise me. He seemed too young to be a teacher, he wore chinos, a dusky blue shirt with a buttoned down collar, and he had very short, curly hair. He was carrying a set of plays.

'You'll all need one of these,' he said. 'Neil – will you hand them out?'

The boy next to me got up and took the plays. He distributed them, giving me a copy first. I stole a glance at him again. I think it was his eyes that had made that impact on me – heavily lidded, rather shy, brown eyes.

I had to remind myself I was actually there for a serious reason, which was to impress everyone with my thespian skills. I found one of Sheila Birling's speeches that I'd been practising last night, and looked at it again. Meanwhile, the drama teacher was moving around the studio, making a list of the people who had turned up. Finally he came to me.

'I don't think I know you.'

'That's because I'm new. You took me to the staff room on the first day. I'm Jac Elliot, 11J.'

'The girl from Chillingham?'

I nodded, hoping he wouldn't make an issue of it.

He grinned at me. 'Very pleased to meet you. I'm your English lit teacher, Mr Jennings.'

I grinned back. I was due to have my first literature lesson that afternoon. Now I was looking forward to it more than ever – Rachel would be eaten up with envy.

'So you're interested in drama?' he asked me.

'Very. I love acting.'

'Do you know *An Inspector Calls*?'

'Yes. We did it at school last year. In English. We spent far too long on it as there was so much to discuss.'

'Sounds like you're going to be very useful.'

He went on and showed me the pieces he wanted me to read. I could feel the adrenalin kicking in. I loved having the opportunity to prove myself, and even though I was slightly shy in normal social situations, I knew that when I was on the stage all that went, and I was different, a chameleon Jac, who could be anyone she wanted.

I watched intently as one by one the other people got up and read from the play. I could tell that a number of them weren't very good. They didn't really understand what they were reading, or they gabbled. The short boy read well, however. He seemed aware of the audience. I watched with even more interest when the dark-haired boy – Neil – walked up the few steps to the stage.

I could have predicted it – he was wonderful. He had a deep, chocolaty voice and the sort of self-possession that makes other people believe in you. If I were Mr Jennings I would have given him a part straight away. I glanced at the teacher, and he was jotting down some notes on a pad. Then he called my name.

I took a deep breath. I breathed out Jac Elliot, fifteen, slightly spotty, raw new recruit, and breathed in Sheila Birling, confident, very middle class, thrilled at her forthcoming marriage to the affluent and charming Gerald Croft. I mounted the stage, held the script in front of me, and spoke the words.

It seemed to be over in an instant. Soon I was climbing down from the stage to rejoin the other would-be performers.

'That was good,' Neil whispered to me.

Oh, bliss! I blushed now, muttered thanks, and decided there and then to have a crush on Neil. Not one of your everyday crushes, where you just write his name on your pencil case and watch it get more and more eroded, but a gigantic crush, the sort that goes down in the history books. I felt supremely happy, savoured the moment, and then began to look forward to ringing Rachel and reliving the whole audition and describing Neil in glorious, technicolour detail. She wouldn't mind. It wouldn't be boasting exactly, because nothing had actually happened to me – yet.

Mr Jennings stood up and told us he'd let us know as soon as possible who'd got the parts. He explained that the play would be put on at the end of term, a matinée for years 9, 10 and 11, and two evening performances for parents and friends. A bell went, and we all prepared to go. I looked at Neil but he was talking to his friends.

I was fizzing with excitement, like a bottle of lemonade when you unscrew the top for the first time. I almost skipped along the corridor and gave a cheery 'hi!' to the people in my form room. Leanne and Claire returned my greeting.

English was in our form room, so there was no need to move. I settled down at my desk and watched people drift out. Not everyone did English literature GCSE, and there were two sets. I turned round and saw that Lisa had remained in the room – she was obviously in my set. Claire had also stayed behind with a friend of hers, Rashmi. They were sitting in a threesome.

'Can I join you?' I asked. It was a bit forward, but my burst of confidence from the auditions hadn't yet deserted me.

'If you like,' Lisa said.

I moved my things and went to sit next to Rashmi. I was still bubbling with excitement. I just had to tell someone where I'd been. 'I've been to the *An Inspector Calls* auditions,' I told them.

'Auditions?' Claire repeated.

'Yeah. *An Inspector Calls*. It's one of my favourite plays. Do you know a boy in our year called Neil? With dark hair and gorgeous eyes?'

'Neil Cooper,' Claire said, and shot Lisa a glance.

'He was there, too. I'd be dead chuffed if I got a part. It was Mr Jennings who's producing. He's cute, isn't he?'

'Not bad,' Claire said, and Rashmi giggled.

'What happens after auditions?' I asked. 'Are the parts posted up somewhere, or do you get told? Have any of you been in a play before?'

'What used to happen at *Chillingham*?' Lisa threw a dangerous emphasis on the word 'Chillingham'.

I decided to ignore her sarcasm. I was bigger than that. 'There was a drama notice board,' I explained, 'opposite the school office. They put up the cast list there. Last year we did *A Midsummer Night's Dream* and me and my friend

Rachel were in that.'

'What were you?' Lisa asked.

'I was Helena and Rachel was Hermia.'

'Hermia? Don't you need an operation for one of those?'

Claire and Rashmi sniggered at Lisa's joke. I joined in, but wondered if Lisa was trying to get at me. I felt a bit defensive.

'Hermia and Helena were the heroines in the play. They were cool parts to have – they're best mates and end up fancying the same guys. It's a comedy.'

'By Shakespeare. I know that,' Lisa said.

She made me feel as if I'd been patronising her. I hadn't meant to, but she seemed determined to pick at what I was saying, and put the worst possible interpretation on it. Once again, I felt nervous. The back of my neck pricked like an animal being stalked. I would have moved away and sat somewhere else but it was too late. Mr Jennings had come in.

He caught my eye, and smiled at me. Was that a good sign? Then he launched into a welcome back speech and gave a lecture on course work. I didn't listen too closely and instead wondered about his home life. Was he married? Probably. I imagined him married, with a little baby at home. Or maybe he was too young to be married – I couldn't decide. I tried to pay more attention to what he was saying.

'Today I thought we'd look at some poetry. Can you get into groups of four and then I'll hand out a poem for you to talk about. One of you read it aloud, then discuss what you think it's about. Pick out any interesting words or phrases and say what they mean to you. You can write up your notes for homework.'

In an instant he was walking among us, handing out sheets. It was too late. I was in a four with Rashmi, Claire and Lisa. I decided the best policy was to stay as quiet as possible, and just keep my thoughts to myself. It was a shame, as I liked discussing poetry.

'Can I read it?' Claire asked.

Lisa was obviously the one who gave permission. Claire read:

> The Poison Tree
>
> I was angry with my friend:
> I told my wrath, my wrath did end.
> I was angry with my foe:
> I told it not, my wrath did grow.
>
> And I water'd it in fears,
> Night & morning with my tears;
> And I sunned it with smiles,
> And with soft deceitful wiles

Only Claire read, *willies*.

Rashmi shrieked and Lisa gave a half smile. 'Show me,' she said. 'It's not willies, Claire – it's wiles.'

'I prefer willies,' Claire said. There was more laughter. Mr Jennings began to stroll over to us. Claire resumed reading.

> And with soft deceitful *wiles*
>
> And it grew both day and night,
> Till it bore an apple bright;
> And my foe beheld it shine,
> And he knew that it was mine,

And into my garden stole
When the night had veiled the pole:
In the morning glad I see
My foe outstretch'd beneath the tree.

Claire was about to laugh again but Mr Jennings was hovering nearby. He came over to us.

'Lisa Webb,' he said. 'I liked your summer coursework – you wrote a good essay. You have an instinct for literature. Keep it up. Only don't get behind this year, OK?'

Lisa looked down at the desk and almost seemed to blush. Then she looked up at him and smiled. I hadn't seen her smile like that before. Up till now she'd struck me as supercool, the way that some girls are. Now she looked a lot more natural. I could tell she liked Mr Jennings. I didn't blame her.

'OK,' he said, leaving us. 'See what you make of the poem.'

The three girls looked at each other. I'd read the poem before. It was by someone called Blake. My mother liked him, that was why I'd heard of him. So I had some ideas about it, but I'd learnt enough by now to keep quiet.

Claire looked at the poem. 'I don't get it,' she said.

'Willies,' Rashmi whispered and they all laughed again.

Claire said, 'What does wrath mean?'

Rashmi replied, 'Wrath is, like, anger, isn't it? So he's saying that . . .' Her voice trailed away.

'It's like a tree,' Lisa intervened. 'He's saying his anger is like a tree, and he's watering it, and it grows, and then it poisons his enemy. So he gets his own way in the end.'

'Oh, right,' Claire said.

Then there was silence.

'Aren't you doing any work?' Lisa said to me.

I felt my stomach tighten. What did I do now? If I stayed quiet, she'd have a go at me. If I said something, she'd make a comment. I began to panic. Then I thought that if I explained the poem and they were able to crib off me and get decent marks, it might help the situation. They would find me useful. That had to be a good thing. Once again I was too desperate to please. I'd passed over the fact that Lisa was smart enough to understand the poem. I hate to admit it, but Chillingham had made me into a bit of a snob.

'I think the poem's really about resentment. How if you sit on your bad feelings they can become poisonous and destroy. The apple is a symbol of resentment. It reminds me a bit of the apple in the Garden of Eden.'

Suddenly Mr Jennings was with us again. 'That's interesting, Jac. Explain yourself.'

'Well, both apples destroy, don't they? And just like the devil in the Garden of Eden is evil, so is the speaker in the poem. He's glad his enemy is dead.'

'Good,' he said, warmly approving. 'I can see you'll be a welcome addition to our class. What did you think of the poem, Lisa.'

''S all right,' she said.

'Just all right?'

Suddenly Lisa smiled at me. 'I agree with Jac,' she said, and went on:

> And I sunned it with smiles,
> And soft deceitful wiles...

'OK. And by the way, Jac, you've got the part of Sheila Birling, if you want it.'

Did I want it? 'Brill!' I said.

He moved away again, leaving a trail of Calvin Klein Be in his wake.

Excitement overwhelmed me. I couldn't suppress my pleasure and I grinned fit to bust.

I should have noticed then that nobody said well done.

Six

When I got home, as soon as Mum answered the door, I began to tell her about the audition. I babbled on as I slung my backpack in the hall, marched into the kitchen and opened the fridge to see what there was to eat.

I was halfway through making a cheese sandwich when it occurred to me that Mum wasn't saying much. I thought she'd be pleased I was in the play, and instead she'd barely acknowledged my ramblings. Holding the knife in midair, I turned to check her out. I could see now that she looked strained and pale. It was as if someone had pulled the plug on my pleasure and it all slowly drained away. Since my gran died a year ago Mum had turned more and more to me for support. It was flattering, being treated like an adult in that respect, but hard, too, because I could feel my mother's pain. Even though she could be difficult at times, she was still my mum. And I loved her. That's why I hated seeing her miserable, and I had a sinking feeling when I noticed her expression that night. I knew she was about to come to me for consolation again.

'What's up?' I asked her.

'Nothing in particular.'

I hate it when people say that, when you know something is wrong. 'Tell me,' I insisted.

'It's only to do with work.'

'Please tell me,' I repeated, completing my sandwich. I took a mouthful of it, as I leant against the work surface.

'It really is nothing, Jac. There was a staff meeting this morning. Apparently we haven't met student target numbers and there's going to have to be fewer A Level groups. It means I might lose a class.'

I swallowed what I was eating. 'But surely that's a good thing? You work much too hard. It'll be nice for you to have some spare time.'

'The money, Jac!'

My parents were always worrying about money. Even before Dad lost his job, money was an issue. It was like an elderly relative we had to consult before we did anything. *Yes, that's all very well, but what about money?* Now it was more like an implacable god. It came first.

'I don't mind spending less,' I said, though not in a very positive voice.

'If it was only a little money I suppose we could manage, but what if they get rid of me altogether?'

Her voice was sounding suspiciously shaky and I was scared she was going to cry. I hated it when my mother cried. She always told me not to worry, she cried easily, that was her temperament, and look how quickly she cheered up afterwards! What she didn't realise was how much it went through me. I was desperate to make her cheer up and tried all the positive ideas I could think of.

'I'm certain they won't get rid of you. You're one of the best teachers in the college. Dad losing his job has made you nervous, that's all.'

'I suppose so, but I just know my head of department would like to me to go.'

'It's not up to her,' I reminded her. 'That's the principal's decision.' Over the years, Mum has told me a lot about the workings of her college. She didn't get on with her head of department. 'And what about all the classes you've carried on from last year? No one else can teach those.'

My mother visibly cheered up. If only I were as good at sorting my own problems as I was hers. I gave Lisa and her gang a fleeting thought. I was glad the crisis with my mother seemed to be averted. Mum didn't actually cry, and I began to feel better.

I suppose we have a strange relationship, my mum and me. She worries about me a lot, I know, but she also tries to treat me as her best friend. I think this is because I'm an only daughter, and Gran always brought her up to keep her troubles in the family. She has friends, but they're not that close. She feels it's OK to tell me stuff, even if it's stuff I don't want to hear. I'm more like my dad and prefer to keep my problems to myself – I reckon I use drama to express my emotions. My mum's a drama queen in real life!

That thought cheered me up, partly because it made me laugh, and partly because it reminded me of the audition again. I made my mum sit down in the living-room and listen to an in-between-mouthfuls-of-cheese-sandwich account of exactly what had happened. I carefully omitted any mention of Neil – I was saving all the really meaty stuff for Rachel. Mum began to smile, and I reckoned that her situation at work couldn't be that bad, if she could come round that quickly. I checked my watch. I would ring Rach at six, when it was cheaper. I couldn't risk Dad coming home before six and finding me on the phone to her, not after last night when we were talking for over an hour. He went demented. Perhaps this time I'd get her to ring me back halfway through.

As soon as I heard the intro to the six o'clock news I raced down from my bedroom and dialled Rachel's number. Both my parents were sitting in front of the telly, – they're news addicts. Gently I closed the living-room door so the noise of the TV wouldn't disturb me, and I sat down on the floor by the little table with the telephone on it, making myself comfortable.

I dialled her number.

She was a long time in coming to the phone. In the meantime I was daydreaming, imagining Rach coming along to some of the rehearsals, if we had to rehearse on a Saturday, and then she could meet the boys. We could all go out for a pizza afterwards, and Neil would offer to pay for mine, I would refuse, but it would be a sign, and then . . . She really was taking a long time to answer the phone. I was about to hang up when suddenly the ringing stopped, and Rachel's mother answered.

'Is Rachel there?'

'Jac? Look – let me speak to your mother – no – it's

46

all right – but you can't speak to Rachel – she's not very well right now.'

'Not well? What's wrong?' I asked urgently.

'Just bad stomach pains. We've called out the doctor but Derek says we ought to take her to casualty.'

'To casualty?'

'We think it might be appendicitis but we can't be sure, not without someone examining her – yes, I won't be long, Derek! – I can't talk now as she's in a lot of pain. I'll ring as soon as we know something, honey. I must go.'

I went numb. The news of Rachel's illness hit me like a slap in the face, and Rachel being ill was as bad as me being ill – worse – I felt so powerless. Powerless, upset and scared. Trembling, I replaced the receiver on the hook. What if it wasn't appendicitis, but something worse? It was terrible to think that something like this could happen. I rushed into the living-room, white as a sheet.

'Rachel's ill,' I stammered.

My parents could see from my face that it was serious. My father clicked on the remote to turn the TV off.

'They think it's appendicitis. They're taking her to hospital.'

I wished I could cry. Perhaps it would make me feel better, and take away the leaden weight in my stomach, aching and dragging me down.

My mother rushed over and hugged me, though her hug didn't seem to have any relevance to the situation Rachel was in.

'If it's appendicitis there's nothing to worry about. They'll whip her appendix out in no time, and she'll be as right as rain.'

'But what if it isn't appendicitis?'

My mother hushed me, stroking my hair. 'It won't be anything serious. If it came on suddenly, it'll go suddenly. Rachel is a healthy girl – she'll be fine.'

I heard my mother's words but they didn't permeate my misery. All the trivia of my day, the boy I fancied, the audition, my English lesson, all of it faded into insignificance. If Rachel was seriously ill, then none of it mattered. Please, please, let her be all right.

'She'll be fine,' my mother crooned, as if in answer to my unspoken prayer. 'She'll be fine.'

Seven

Rachel had faced the surgeon's knife, and I was about to face double aerobics.

Rachel's dad had rung from the hospital as I was getting ready for bed, to say that the diagnosis of appendicitis was confirmed, and they would operate as soon as a surgeon was available. There was also a message from Rachel to me, demanding I visit as soon as possible. Everyone told me there was nothing to worry about. I kind of believed them.

I tried to imagine what had happened to Rachel last night, as I walked along the games block corridor. I saw her being wheeled along on a hospital trolley with a nurse and an orderly on either side. When I pushed open the door to the girls' changing area, I almost expected to see the drips, machine dials and tubes of the operating theatre.

But it was just the changing rooms. There were wire-cage lockers all around, and rows of pegs. The walls were bare brick, and someone had scrawled graffiti in black pen. It looked as if the caretakers hadn't been able to erase the words, they were still legible, grey and smeared. There were no windows in the room, just bright, fluorescent lighting and the whirring of a fan, which only seemed to spread the sweaty, thick smell around the room. I resolved to get changed and out of there as quickly as possible.

I walked past the middle section of lockers and saw Lisa, Leanne, Jodie and Claire sitting on a bench along the wall.

'Look who's here,' Lisa said.

I wanted to pretend to myself that her comment wasn't meant to intimidate me. I decided to ignore her tone of voice and make out she was being friendly. The business with Rachel had had an odd effect on me – I'd learned there were more important things than Lisa's low-level snipes.

'Hi!' I said, as cheerfully as I could.

No one replied. I felt Lisa watching me and it made me uneasy. More so than usual, because I was about to get changed. No one likes to be looked at when they're taking their clothes off. So I didn't start immediately, hoping she'd turn her eyes elsewhere. I got my games blouse, shorts and trainers out of my bag, fumbling a bit, feeling self-conscious. When I turned round, Lisa was still watching me.

My first impulse was to ask her what the hell she was doing, but I was scared of a confrontation. So I just moved out of the line of her vision and then began to unbutton my shirt. As more girls came into the changing rooms the tension seemed to diffuse. So when Jodie giggled, I couldn't be sure what she was laughing at. Quickly I wriggled into my games blouse. Had I put my bra on inside out? Was that why they were laughing? I could see out of the corner of my eye that they were still staring at me. I could ignore it no longer. Feeling desperate, I turned and faced them, but tried to sound as noncommittal as possible.

'Hey, you lot! Quit staring at me, else I won't take off my skirt.' I thought making a joke of it would help – talk about naïve!

'Who'd want to look at *you*?' It was as if I'd fed her the line.

Her comment stung me. Was there something wrong with the way I looked? My body? The clothes I was wearing? Something else? The teasing was getting more specific now, and as it did, I felt worse, more targeted, more vulnerable. With my back to them, I unzipped my skirt and put on my shorts. I slipped off my shoes and began to lace up my trainers.

'Nobody likes her,' I heard Leanne say, clear as a bell. 'Everyone says she's a sad old snob. Really up herself. And desperate to pull.'

'Nobody in their right mind would want to pull her. Fat arse.'

Jodie laughed at Lisa's remark.

I felt the blood rush to my face. Even though they hadn't mentioned my name, I knew they were talking about me. I didn't have the courage to turn around and face them. I was on my own, I was new, and I was seriously outnumbered. The best I could hope for right now was that the comments would stop. Maybe if I showed them their words didn't bother me, they would leave me alone. Perhaps they only wanted a reaction – yes, that was it. I would ignore them. Do nothing. Stay unprovoked, cool. I shoved all my clothes on to the peg and my shoes into the wire locker and, holding my head high, walked out of the changing rooms.

They were only comments. Sticks and stones may break my bones, the saying goes, but words can never harm me. I thought it was my weakness to be so upset by the comments they had made. I resolved to be stronger.

I entered the gym, feeling safe again, as the teacher was there. She was wearing a Nike tracksuit, and loud dance music was ricocheting around the walls. The teacher acknowledged me and I smiled back. Gradually the gym filled with girls dressed in baggy T-shirts and shorts. I cringed as I realised I was the only one in an aertex games blouse. I hated Mum for insisting I reused my Chillingham games gear – I felt such an idiot.

'Ready for the warm-up, girls?' the teacher said.

I didn't dare look round to see if Lisa and her mates had arrived. I watched the teacher adjust the level of the music, and then she began to march gently up and down on the spot. I copied her, trying not to think of what had happened in the changing rooms. Maybe all new girls got that treatment – it was a kind of initiation rite. Better than having your head shoved down a toilet. Perhaps I was overreacting because I was still all het up over Rachel. Think positive, I told myself, things might get better. The teacher stepped out to the right in a grapevine manoeuvre, and I had to concentrate to get it right.

I wondered why I assumed Lisa was the one behind it

all? Jodie, Leanne and Claire were just as bad, yet it was Lisa who bothered me. Instinctively I knew she was the ringleader. She had some kind of power – if I could identify what it was, maybe I would understand her better. She looked right, that was for sure. Her uniform was always untidy but her face was immaculate, even sophisticated. She wore foundation, blusher, lipstick and mascara. Everyone treated her as if she mattered, even the teachers, who either picked on her all the time, or side-stepped her, praising wherever they could. I thought that if Lisa approved of me, I'd be free to be myself and make my own friends. But clearly she didn't . . .

Fortunately, I had to stop thinking. We'd got to the serious bit of the aerobics session. We were jumping, flinging our arms about and there was a demonic glee in the eyes of the games teacher. Me and Rach always used to say that you had to be a sadist to want to be a games teacher. That, and a hypocrite. They took us out on to the hockey field in the freezing cold while they were wrapped from head to foot in designer tracksuits.

Only this teacher was no hypocrite. She was working as hard as we were. I joined in as energetically as I could, and tried to think about how fit I was getting. Before I knew it, it was time for the stretches. They felt good. And then the session was over.

'OK, girls, go and get changed. Except for Lisa Webb. I want to know why you haven't signed up for netball practice.'

Hearing that, I ran to the changing rooms and got dressed as quickly as I could while Lisa was out of the way. I spared a thought for Rachel, however, and wondered if she was comfortable now, and had been able to have breakfast. I decided to ring her as soon as I could.

That thought cheered me up. Once I knew she was all right I'd feel a whole lot better. I left the changing rooms as Lisa and her friends came in from the gym. They ignored me, and I was confident I'd survived the worst.

As soon as it was lunchtime I ran out of school to the shops, where I knew there was a telephone box. Luckily it was in working order. I got out my phonecard and dialled Rachel's home number. It rang for ages, but there was no reply.

I wasn't defeated that easily. I rang the operator and asked for the number of the hospital. I got through, tracked down the right ward, and with a beating heart asked the nurse how Rachel was.

'Rachel Jones? Yes, she was operated on last night.'

'Can I speak to her?'

'The doctor's with her right now. Shall I pass you on to one of her parents? They're around somewhere.'

I waited impatiently. Rachel's mum came on the line and assured me that the operation was a success, although Rach's appendix had been badly inflamed and they got it out in the nick of time. Rachel had been a bit edgy going into theatre, but she was fine now. It was probably not a good idea for me to visit tonight, but maybe the next day.

Relief washed over me. The nightmare was over and life was back to normal again. It was weird, how quickly things could change. Who would have guessed even last week that Rach would be rushed into hospital? Now she'd had her operation and was recovering. I remembered what my mother had said, and had to admit she was right. Things that happened suddenly were over suddenly. Things that began more gradually stayed around for a while.

As I came out of the telephone booth I spotted Lisa and co queuing outside the chippy. They hadn't noticed me, so I sneaked round the back of the box and headed back to school. I had some sandwiches with me and ate them as I walked along. I wished I had someone to talk to.

I checked my watch and saw there were still forty minutes or so before afternoon registration. What could I do with myself? If I hung around school, I might collide with Lisa again. No one else seemed to want to come near me. Then I had a brilliant idea. I would check out the school library. It was weird that I hadn't been there before because, as I said earlier, I like reading, and the atmosphere in libraries is always relaxing. Anyway, I could maybe get a start on my maths homework and free up the evening. There were also my lines in the play to learn.

Pleased to have something concrete to do, I made straight for the library. It was OK and I knew I'd be safe in there. There were windows all along one wall, letting in lots of light, and reading tables by the windows. There were posters, magazines in racks and a display of photographs of a recent exchange visit to France. The librarian didn't notice me come in, as she was busy cataloguing books. I felt a little lonely, as if nobody really cared whether I was at Markfield or not.

I walked over to the empty end table in front of the reference books. I took what I needed from my bag, sat down and glanced at the other people around me. On the next table, facing me, but with his head deep in a book, was Neil. My stomach did a backflip. He hadn't noticed me, but I was pleased, because that gave me time to straighten my hair and cool down a bit. I hoped there weren't any stray crumbs of egg sandwich decorating my face.

I opened my maths textbook and then my exercise book. The numbers could have been hieroglyphics for all they meant to me. Still, I was glad I had them on the table because they acted as a sort of decoy. I put the date in my book and copied out the title of the homework, occasionally shooting quick, surreptitious glances at Neil. At about glance number four, our eyes met.

He recognised me immediately and grinned. Then he went back to his work. I tried to see what he was doing – I couldn't tell what he was reading. I attempted my maths again – fine chance! My brain had completely stopped functioning. I put my maths away and got out my copy of *An Inspector Calls* and thought I'd look at that instead. I scanned the first page, then eyed Neil again. I could see now that he was also reading the play. It didn't take an inspector to work out he had been given a part too. But which one?

Overcome with curiosity, I reasoned there was nothing stopping me going over and asking him – he didn't know I fancied him like mad. Or did he? At times like this you really need a mate to help you suss out the situation. But it was a free country, and girls were allowed to start innocent conversations with lads. So I sidled over.

'Have you got a part?' I asked.

'Gerald Croft,' he replied.

'I'm Sheila Birling.'

'How do you do, Sheila Birling?'

'Very well, thank you.' I tried to put on a Sheila Birling voice. It was easier like that, not being me. He took the bait.

'I believe we're engaged,' he said in a toffee-nosed Gerald Croft voice.

I wanted to keep it up, but couldn't. 'We are engaged,' I replied in my normal voice, 'but I break it off when I discover you've had an affair with Eva Smith.'

'That's heartless of you,' he joked.

'You deserved it,' I hit back. I was beginning to enjoy myself.

'But you're not so wonderful yourself. You got Eva Smith sacked.'

Interesting to find out he knew the play. 'Yes, but I was sorry afterwards for what I did.'

He laughed. Neil had a lovely laugh, a sort of rich chuckle. It made me more aware of him, and less of the parts we'd been playing. Neither of us said anything for a moment, both suddenly self-conscious.

'Hey,' Neil said. 'I'm going to enjoy acting with you. You certainly know how to get into a part.'

'So do you,' I said, returning the compliment swiftly.

'Are you finding your lines difficult to learn? Here – sit down.'

He pushed the chair next to him back. I took it.

'I haven't really started yet. Other things got in the way. My best friend's in hospital.'

'Is it serious?' He looked concerned.

'She had her appendix removed. I've just rung the hospital and spoken to her mum. She's OK now. She's coming round from the anaesthetic. I've been worried about her all morning.'

'I bet. My sister's baby was in intensive care when he was born and we were all totally stressed out.'

He was sensitive and caring, too! I couldn't believe my

57

luck. 'Is the baby all right?' I remembered to ask.

'Sure – that was a year ago.'

'I'm going to see Rachel tomorrow. That is, if she's well enough. She's in the kids' hospital, even though she's fifteen. For her sake, I hope she isn't on a ward full of toddlers.'

Neil laughed again. His laugh made my knees go weak.

'Do I know your friend?' he asked. 'I don't think I know you.'

'That's because I'm new. I'm Jac Elliot.'

'Jac,' he said. 'Your name suits you.'

I loved the way he said that. I just smiled inanely at him.

'Why did you come here?'

My instinct told me I could tell Neil the truth. For the first time since I started at Markfield, I had found someone I could open up to. 'It's a long story. I used to go to Chillingham Girls', but my dad lost his job and my parents couldn't afford the fees. I didn't really mind moving schools, except I miss Rachel.'

He nodded sympathetically. 'It can be tough changing schools. But this place is all right. The drama's good. Last Christmas we put on a panto for the local primary school. I was Widow Twankey.'

I began to laugh. It was the thought of the delectable Neil dressed up in a washerwoman's clothes with his cheeks pinked up. He began to laugh, too. That made me feel even more giggly and I was afraid I'd begin to splutter.

'Sshhh!' warned the librarian, glancing at us meaningfully. We continued to talk in a whisper.

'I'm in year 11,' Neil offered.

'Me too. I haven't seen you in any of my classes.'

'Yeah, it's a big school.'

'Yeah.'

There was silence. Each of us had run out of things to say. I didn't want to sit there like a wally, searching for conversation, so I decided to make my exit.

'I'm going to have to make a start on my lines,' I said.

'Yeah. Me too.'

I got up. 'See ya.'

'See you around,' he said.

I went back to my seat and opened my copy of the play. Rather than learn my lines, I rehearsed what we had just said to each other, and pieced together what I'd found out about him. He was my age, my wavelength, dead sensitive, even better looking close up than I'd remembered, he had a great sense of humour – he was perfect, and therefore far too good for me. But that didn't stop me fancying him.

I tried to work out what he thought of me. He was friendly, smiled a lot, and even pulled out a chair for me, which proved he wanted my company. But when I went, he just said see you around, which was very casual. I had to tell myself that I still hardly knew him – he might have a steady girlfriend, or he might be the sort of boy who just flirted and then backed off. I couldn't wait to discuss him with Rachel.

Once again I tried to study my lines, trying not to look at Neil or, if I did, to pretend to be looking elsewhere and catch him accidentally out of the corner of my eye. I just couldn't concentrate while he was there. In some ways it was a relief when the bell went and we were able to wave goodbye to each other.

I was thinking of Neil all the way back to the form

room. The room was empty when I got there, and I was about to put my bag down on the desk when Mr Weston arrived.

'Jac – could you give me a hand? I've been nabbed to take some books to the English stock room. You'd think one of the English department would see to it,' he muttered.

'Sure,' I said, pleased not to have to be there when Lisa and her gang arrived.

I followed him down to reception through masses of kids pushing their way to the classrooms. There were three boxes piled up on the coffee-table and Mr Weston passed one to me.

'Can you manage this, Jac?'

I nodded and adjusted my grip on the box. It was an awkward shape but not too heavy. At that moment the boys' games teacher walked through reception in his tracksuit.

'Are you going to the match tonight?' he asked Mr Weston.

Mr Weston said he was, and then they began some typical male chit-chat about their team's chances. My mum told me once that that was how men socialised. Still feeling blissed out from my chat with Neil, I decided to be tolerant of Mr Weston, even though he'd left me holding a box of books.

Eventually he remembered I was there, apologised profusely, picked up the other two boxes himself, and we made our way back to the form room. The stock room was next to it. We placed the boxes on the table in the middle of the room and went back next door. My bag was still on the desk where I had left it.

Mr Weston raced through the register. I felt compelled to look and see if Lisa was there, and she was, but she wasn't looking at me. That had to be a good sign. Perhaps she'd had her fun and was finished with me. On the way to double chemistry I fell into step with Rashmi, and she was quite friendly. In fact, I followed her to the back bench of the lab and we sat together.

The chemistry teacher was one of those witterers, the sort that go on about anything but their subject. They're great, because all you have to do is suss out what they really want to talk about and ask them questions about it, and they're off. Some of the girls were asking her about her baby son, and she was saying how they took him to a theme park or something, but I wasn't really listening.

Then suddenly I picked up the words 'covalent bonding' and realised she'd got back on to chemistry again.

'Get out your notebooks,' the teacher said. 'I want you to copy this down.'

'You've got our notebooks, Miss,' someone piped up.

'Oh, of course I have. They're in the prep room.'

She vanished to get them and I decided to open my bag to get out my pencil case.

I untied the knot and pulled open the cords. There was something there that hadn't been there before. A tampon – a used tampon – or had they just made it look used? I didn't know. I felt sick to the pit of my stomach and quickly closed my bag before anyone could see.

Was it a mistake? Could it just have fallen in? I didn't want to believe the evidence of my own eyes. I knew who had put it there.

'Here's your book, Jac,' the teacher said. 'A good start.'

I hardly heard her. I was still stunned, still trying to make sense of what I'd seen. It was Lisa's idea of a joke. It wasn't a joke – it was plain nasty, revolting. I was shaking with anger, with disgust, with fear – or maybe with all three.

The teacher was writing something on the blackboard and I knew if I didn't start copying it down someone would notice something was wrong. I whispered to Rashmi that I needed to borrow a pen and she pushed one over to me.

I forced myself to copy what was on the board, but my mind was in overdrive. I couldn't bear to think of what was in my bag, and couldn't face having to get rid of it. I felt like I wanted to throw my whole bag away; maybe I would – maybe I would just say to Mum that I'd left it on the bus. Only it was new, and she'd be upset.

Ought I to tell her the truth? I began to imagine how hysterical she'd be, and the scene we'd have, and her saying it was her fault, she should never have moved me from Chillingham. The thought of all the histrionics made me cringe. Surely I was old enough now to deal with this business myself? If I didn't think about it too closely I could just pick up the disgusting thing and throw it away.

I wondered briefly about telling a teacher, but it would be so embarrassing. I certainly couldn't show anyone my bag, and if I didn't they might not believe me, they might think I was making it up. Also, there was no evidence connecting it to Lisa. Then if I said it was her, and she knew I'd grassed on her, next time she might do something worse. I felt trapped. It was like I was in a maze, and each time I turned to find an exit, I came across another dead end. Perhaps I ought to leave off thinking about it. And that was what I did. I forced myself to concentrate on my chemistry, and kicked my bag away from me. I was strong; I wasn't giving in to Lisa. She wasn't going to get a reaction from me, any sort of reaction. I thought I could deal with her on my own. Jac the Giant Killer. As if...

Eight

Along the corridor to ward nine someone had painted a series of dancing dinosaurs, all grinning stupidly, looking as if they'd had too much to drink. They were there to cheer the kids up, and they made me laugh, too. Once I was into the ward area there were the usual health posters and nurses' offices, and then the ward proper, with beds lined up on either side.

I held my breath. It was partly the smell of illness and antiseptic but also because I was always slightly nervous whenever I was about to see sick people. I hoped no one was really ill. As I entered the ward, I forced myself to focus just on where Rachel was. I didn't see her, but caught sight of her mother, who was leaning over her, saying something. Rachel's bed was right at the end which, meant I had to walk all the way down the ward to it.

Eyes straight ahead, I told myself. I still couldn't help

glimpsing someone to the left of me who was on a drip, sound asleep, curled into the foetal position. Someone else looked pale and distant, staring at nothing. One bed, most sinister of all, had curtains around it – bright curtains with teddy bears all over them. There were small children running about, and then there was Rachel. Her hair was a bit lank and she was wearing an unfamiliar nightie, but otherwise she looked just like Rachel. I smiled at her and held out the box of Milk Tray I'd brought, feeling embarrassed, seeing her out of context like that.

'Jac!' exclaimed her mother. 'It's so good of you to come.'

Parents are always doing things like that, thanking you for visiting your best mate. As if you needed thanking! Anyway, I had a lot to tell Rachel, so I was partly visiting her for selfish reasons. I told Mrs Jones that my mother was in the coffee bar and wanted to speak to her.

'I'd love a coffee,' Rachel's mum said. 'I'll just leave you two to it, shall I?'

Rachel nodded rather too enthusiastically. While Mrs Jones was getting her things together I looked round again. Poor old Rach! It must have felt like someone had transported her back to playgroup. The ward was full of stuff like jigsaws, Lego, shape sorters and picture books. There were some Sony PlayStations but some determined small boys had commandeered those. I couldn't see any patients of Rachel's age at all.

Eventually Mrs Jones succeeded in locating all her things and departed, leaving me with Rachel. Unaccountably I felt overcome with shyness. I think it was because we had been thrust into this strange situation. I noticed the get-well cards and a plastic jug of orange squash on her bedside cabinet, and some magazines at the foot of her bed. By the side of her bed was a white board with her name and age written on it, and the name of a nurse.

'How are you?'

Rachel grimaced. 'Still sore. Sort of uncomfortable inside. But I'll be able to go home soon.'

'Lucky you. You'll miss loads of school.'

'Would you believe, one of the teachers rang Dad to ask if I wanted any work!'

'Can't they even leave you alone in here?'

We both laughed. Suddenly I wished I was Rachel. How much easier it would be if I was recovering from appendicitis, rather than having to face Lisa again. And when she was better, she would just go back to Chillingham. While I...

Rachel smiled at me, and I attempted to smile back. I wondered if I ought to tell her now what I'd found in my school bag. Though I often teased her about it, Rachel was brilliant at solving other people's problems, especially mine. Having decided not to bother my parents, and not to involve any teachers, Rachel was the only person left I could speak to. Only I'd kept the business to myself for a while now, so it was surprisingly difficult to find the right words. And where should I begin? I'd deliberately said so little to Rachel about Markfield that I would have to start from the first day.

'Rach – ' I began.

'I'll tell you what the worst thing was – '

We had spoken simultaneously, and then laughed together, too.

'You first.'

'No, you.'

'Oh, all right,' Rachel said. 'The worst thing was when they came for me to go into theatre. Even though I was in agony, I'd got this idea into my head that if I had a general anaesthetic, I'd never wake up! And I was all spaced out from the stuff they gave me to drink to calm me down. So I was panicking, and the nurse had to spend all her time reassuring me. She's ever so nice – her name is Ann.'

'So then what happened?' I realised Rachel needed to talk about what she'd been through. I preferred to let her do that, and leave my problems till later.

'They wheeled me out on a trolley, which was even more scary, and took me into the room outside theatre and I was surrounded by nurses and other people, and this bloke in a gown said I'd feel my arm going cold first of all – the funny thing was I didn't feel that, but my head went all heavy – and then the next thing was I felt someone pulling on my arm saying, Rachel, wake up Rachel, and I opened my eyes – and like, wow! – there were two gorgeous men standing over me – honestly, Jac, some of the best-looking men I've ever seen work in this place! The anaesthetist was dreamy and my surgeon was...'

If Rach was leching after men again, then she was completely back to normal! I was glad. Now I didn't want to spoil her pleasure at having survived a scary operation by landing my problems on her. It seemed mean – mean and selfish. Maybe I would wait until she was out of hospital. She was still rabbiting on, and I was only half listening to her.

'...the nurses are lovely and ever so kind and stop to chat even though they work so hard. That nurse over there is getting married next month. Her boyfriend is a footballer, which is *so* cool. And Ann, my nurse, is actually a grandmother although she doesn't look old enough. The little boy in the bed opposite me has been very poorly. He had some sort of virus, which made him swell up, and he cried all of last night. His mother was going mad. He shouldn't be in our ward, which is surgical, but they ran out of beds...'

I stole a glance across at him. He was still red and blotchy. I began to wonder what was wrong with the other kids in the ward and to realise how awful it must be to be ill. I felt guilty about wishing I had appendicitis. Sitting in the hospital I began to get a sense of proportion about what had happened to me at Markfield. Here there were children with the most dreadful complaints – there were other wards apart from this one – intensive care, oncology – and all the kids there had something serious to worry about. And here was I, all churned up because someone put a tampon in my bag. I was the world's greatest wimp. I decided there and then not to tell Rachel. Compared to her, and all the kids around me, my situation was trivial – and it was over. All I had to remind me of it was a stain on my French book, which I'd covered up with some stickers from a magazine. Covered up. In my mind, I drew curtains around the whole incident, bright curtains with teddy bears all over them. It would remain like that, concealed from view.

There was something else I could tell Rachel, though. 'Rach,' I began, when she'd finally finished talking, 'I think I've fallen in love.'

'How cool is that? Who is he? Does he have a friend?'

'Yeah, loads. His name's Neil – '

'Like Neil Morrissey, from *Men Behaving Badly*!'

'Except he's not like that at all, but all sweet and sensitive. And he's a dead good actor. I met him the first time at the auditions and...' As I chatted on, I began to feel better. There was no point dwelling on bad things. '... so I think he likes me, but I don't know whether he fancies me!'

'That's the trouble with boys,' Rachel mused. 'You never know what they're thinking – '

'*If* they're thinking,' I joked.

'Look – why don't you give him a sign? I think sometimes lads are more shy than we are. You have to encourage them.'

'Look who's talking!' Rachel would come out with these things that sounded so worldly wise, but if she really fancied someone, she'd clam up completely.

'No, I'm serious. Give him a hint. Or smile at him in a certain way. Make eye contact. Then look away quickly.'

'Where d'you get that from? A manual on flirting?'

'I dare you to try it.'

'Huh!'

Just then Mrs Jones reappeared, with my mum in tow.

'You two seem to be having a good time,' she said, almost as if we weren't supposed to.

'It's nice to see Jac,' Rachel said. I could hear from her voice that perhaps she was getting a little tired.

'Come on, Jac, you don't want to outstay your welcome.' That was my mum, who comes out with the oddest phrases sometimes – phrases I'm sure she learnt from her mother. Nevertheless, I got up from my black plastic seat and began to say my goodbyes. A nurse was walking round the ward, turning some of the lights out, and I realised this was a tactful sign to visitors to be on their way.

I linked arms with my mother as we left the ward. Like Rachel, I was feeling much better.

Nine

'Well done, Sheila! You're very spirited, which is good. But when you look at Gerald, try to show that you're angry, too. When you learn he had a mistress you feel betrayed. It's probably not a good idea to smile at him so much.'

Whoops! I thought to myself – I'd better watch it. Maybe the middle of a rehearsal wasn't the best time to take up Rachel's advice and let Neil know I liked him. I willed myself to stop blushing. Then I had this crazy idea. It would be easy enough to spit fire at Neil if I imagined he was Lisa. I gathered myself together.

'OK,' I said to Mr Jennings. 'I'll give it another shot.'

This time I looked him in the eyes, and if looks could kill, he would have been dead and buried. I hurled my words like missiles. It felt good, highly therapeutic.

'Bravo!' cried Mr Jennings.

'I feel awful now,' whimpered Neil. 'I didn't mean to go off with Eva Smith, honest!'

I laughed and everyone joined in.

'I was only acting. I like you really.' Damn. I'd done it again. I could have kicked myself. I checked out Neil but he just looked his normal, cheerful self. It was hard to tell whether he'd taken the bait, or been terminally embarrassed by me.

For the last week or so during rehearsals, we'd got on well. Most of the time he hung around with Eric Birling, or the boy playing Eric Birling, the one with the wide smile, who I'd earmarked for Rachel. I think he might have been a little shorter than her but that hardly mattered in a good relationship. When Neil was with Eric (real name, Michael) I didn't often go up to speak to them. If Eric wasn't around it was somehow easier to strike up a conversation with Neil. Anyway, it was enough to fuel my daydreams.

In fact, every night, in order to fall asleep, I imagined me and Neil in different situations, but in every situation the words were the same. He would declare his undying love for me and I would confess I felt the same. Then he would kiss me. And then we would meet up with Rachel and Michael and all go on somewhere.

I know daydreaming like that is a little immature, but I needed those daydreams. They helped block out an uncomfortable reality. Things weren't going well at school. Since the tampon incident Lisa hadn't done anything dramatic, but she and her gang gave me dirty looks, walked round me when they saw me in the corridor and avoided me when I was in the classroom. There were also snide remarks and cutting comments. I think I could have coped if it was only them, but people were scared of Lisa, and the rest of the class took her lead. People weren't keen to be seen talking to me. The boys pretended I wasn't there, and it was my biggest fear that some of them might know Neil and slag me off to him. The other girls ignored me, too, except for a few, including Rashmi, and when she talked to me it almost felt as if she was doing it without permission, or because she felt sorry for me.

In some ways, I think that was the worst part of it. When nobody speaks to you, you feel as though you don't exist, as if you don't matter, not in the slightest, which is, I suppose, what bullies want you to think. Then after a time you crave attention from anyone. I never realised just how much you need smiles in the corridor and people saying hello and simply hanging out with you. If it wasn't for the play I don't think I would have coped, or perhaps things would have been brought to a head much sooner.

I tried to work out if it was my fault that no one liked me. I couldn't think of anything I'd done wrong – it wasn't as if I was a child murderer or anything. OK, so I came from a school they thought was posh. That wasn't a crime. Occasionally I said the wrong thing, but I'd never been mean to anyone. Perhaps that was it – I was too soft. Worst of all was the irrational feeling that there was something dreadfully wrong with me as a person, and there was nothing, nothing I could do to alter that, however hard I tried. That was why thinking about Neil cheered me up so much. He seemed to like me, and that thought was my lifeline to sanity in those days. That, and my friendship with Rachel.

★

The rehearsal sadly came to an end as the bell rang.

'Time for registration,' Mr Jennings said, rather reluctantly. 'Come on, Jac. I'm teaching you next. Let's go down to the English block.'

That meant I didn't have another opportunity to talk to Neil. I liked Mr Jennings very much, but wished he was more aware of my growing feelings for Gerald Croft. Smiling to myself, I picked up my bag and followed Mr Jennings down the corridor.

'I think I've made you late for registration,' he said.

'It doesn't matter. Mr Weston's away today. He's on a course.'

'Oh yes – the standardising meeting. I meant to tell you, Jac, I've read your literature coursework from your old school, and it's very good. I liked your essay on *Jane Eyre*. Did you have any help with it?'

'The teacher explained what we had to do, but otherwise, no.'

'Well done.'

I was pleased by his comments but embarrassed and I guess I looked a bit flushed as I walked into the classroom. All the group were there. There was a chair next to Rashmi but she was sitting in front of Lisa, so I looked for somewhere else to sit. A number of the chairs in the classroom had vanished and the only empty space was next to a boy called Simon Woodward, who no one ever sat next to because he had a hygiene problem. But it was better than sitting in front of Lisa.

Actually, the lesson was pretty good. We were doing *Of Mice and Men*, and the time just sped by. We had a really good discussion about the characters, everyone was chipping in with their opinions, and Mr Jennings was a good laugh, too. I forgot my own problems and became thoroughly absorbed in what was going on. The bell caught us all by surprise, and then we started packing up for our next lesson, which in my case was French.

To my surprise, two girls actually came up to speak to me – Katy and Cassie from 11D. They were smiling and seemed friendly. I was cautious, however.

'Are you going to French?' Katy asked.

'Yeah.'

'D'you mind if we walk with you?'

I nodded and we left the form room, our bags swinging over our shoulders.

'Do you like Mr Jennings?' Cassie asked.

'Yeah,' I said. 'He's cool.'

Both Katy and Cassie giggled, which seemed a strange response. I thought everyone liked Mr Jennings – he was one of the popular teachers, and nobody messed around in his lessons. I was puzzled.

'Why?' I asked. 'Don't you like him?'

'Yeah,' Katy said, 'but not as much as *you* do.' They laughed some more and I felt increasingly uneasy. What were they getting at? There was something going on here and I had to find out what it was.

'Why are you laughing?'

My question only made them laugh more. So much so that they had stopped walking, and were creased up, standing there in the corridor with a poster of Rouen behind them.

'What's going on?' I demanded.

'It's just that – we think you ought to know – ' Katy began to pull herself together – 'everyone's saying that you pulled him.'

'Pulled him!' I couldn't believe what I was hearing.

'Yeah. Lisa said they saw you at the cinema last night and you were snogging him and he had his hand up your skirt.'

'WHAT?' I couldn't think what to say I was so taken aback. 'Don't be so stupid. I wasn't even at the cinema.'

'Lisa said you'd deny it. And don't call me stupid. We saw the way you walked in with him this afternoon.'

'We were just talking about my coursework. Look,' I pleaded with her, 'can't you see this is just a daft rumour? I mean, I'm only fifteen and he's probably twice my age.'

Cassie shook her head in disagreement. 'There's a girl in year 9 who went out with my brother and he's twenty-eight.'

'Look. It's not true. OK? It's just not true.'

I don't know whether they believed me then, or felt sorry for tormenting me. For a moment Katy's tone changed – she was warning me now, more as a friend.

'I'd watch it if I were you. Lisa Webb doesn't like you. She's been spreading rumours, telling everyone you're a slag. Everyone believes her.'

'A slag?'

We reached the language labs. I think now I was more angry than anything else. If what Lisa had said about me was true, I think I'd have been upset, but these rumours about me and Mr Jennings showed she was desperate. Me, a slag? It was so ridiculous, it was almost laughable. But I knew the power of rumours, and the idea that everyone thought this of me was infuriating. Worst of all, the rumour might reach Neil's ears. I felt like a tormented animal that had suffered enough and was ready to hit out.

French was over in a blur. I had been working automatically, nursing my anger, determined to confront Lisa. At the end of the lesson I was still mad, though increasingly nervous. My courage was ebbing away, vanishing like sand in an hourglass. I began to think about how best to approach her. If I came over too angry, it might end in a fight and, since I'd never fought before, that scared me. Only if I sounded too placatory, too friendly, I would just be casting myself in the role of victim. Then I thought of Sheila Birling. She had guts, but she had class, too. Maybe I ought to confront Lisa as Sheila Birling; stick up for myself, and put her down. Stupid me. I was still under the illusion that I could handle this myself.

As I walked past the form room, I saw Lisa and Leanne in there with several other girls and some of the boys. No time like the present. My knees felt shaky and my heart was beating nineteen to the dozen. I walked into the room.

I still go cold when I think of that now. I had a feeling that I'd made the wrong decision, and knew I should have just turned and walked out of the room and gone home. But in my own mind I'd committed myself to taking a stand. I begged Sheila Birling to come to my aid. In a shaky voice, I began.

'I don't know what you've been saying about me, Lisa, but I'm here to say none of it is true.'

There was a ripple of laughter. There is no worse sound in the world than people laughing at you.

Lisa challenged me. 'If you don't know what I've been saying about you, how do you know it isn't true?' She was playing with me, like a cat with a mouse.

'That stuff about Mr Jennings,' I said.

'We've all seen you flirting with him, haven't we?' Lisa commented, getting out her lipgloss and expertly applying some.

'I don't flirt with him.'

More laughter. Lisa said, 'Sucking *up* to the teachers isn't all she does.'

There was a snigger of appreciation at Lisa's crude remark. I felt myself getting hot and embarrassed. I hated being the centre of attention in this way. It was me versus the rest of the class and no referee to ensure fair play. I tried to extricate myself from the situation by rising above it all.

'I really don't know what you're talking about!' Sheila Birling would have said that.

'Slag,' whispered Lisa.

The word threw me, toppled me from my Sheila Birling pedestal.

'I'm not a slag.' My voice sounded thin and reedy. I was flailing. I thought perhaps I ought to give as good as I got. Maybe the only way to deal with a bully was on her own terms.

'You're a slag,' I whispered.

'What did you say?'

'You're the slag,' I repeated a little more loudly.

'She called Lisa a slag!' Leanne shouted. 'Did you all hear that? She called you a slag, Lisa.'

'You'll regret that,' Lisa said, cool and deadly.

I didn't know what to say. I was feeling more and more scared by the minute and knew the confrontation had gone hopelessly wrong. Now I just wanted to get out of the classroom without any further loss of dignity, and in one piece.

'Well, maybe neither of us is a slag, then.'

With that, I picked up my bag and walked out, hearing the room erupt as I left. I was drowning in shame, engulfed in embarrassment. How could I have been so dumb as to think I could outwit Lisa? I called her a slag – how stupid was that? And then I took it back at the end, showing myself up as doubly stupid in front of everyone. If they didn't have a reason to bully me before, they certainly did now.

I walked along the corridor until I reached an exit door. I pushed on the bar and left the school building. I walked until I thought no one could see me and then I broke into a run. I wanted to get away from school as quickly as possible. I was surprised at how fast I was running, fuelled by adrenalin, fear and bitter shame.

I ran so fast that I caught the early bus. Only a few first years were on it, eating crisps and drinking Coke. I took a window seat and put my bag on the floor. I felt so humiliated I was numb – I couldn't feel, couldn't cry. It was as if I felt guilty, as if I'd done something to be ashamed of. Somehow the bullying had made me become the person they thought I was – a stuck-up little twerp. They had projected their view of me onto me, and it had stuck. Even I was beginning to believe it. I used to be in a permanent good mood, a laugh at school, a normal person, and now I'd become something different. It was like a kind of insanity, like being brainwashed. But at the time I just felt eaten up with shame and pain.

I think it was the shame that prevented me telling anyone. That, and the feeling that, in some way, it was my fault. Also I wasn't sure what to call what was happening to me. Was it proper bullying? Somehow I'd always imagined that real bullying was different – there was violence involved, or people came round your house and shoved things in your letterbox. I'd read in the papers about extreme cases of bullying, and confused these extremes with the typical. So I discounted what was going on, and turned in on myself. It was easier to deny it – easier to block it out, to tell myself I was on my way home now and nothing else would happen. Even easier to kid myself that maybe my confrontation had worked, and perhaps Lisa might have realised I could stand up for myself.

Meanwhile, I would go home, see how Rachel was, watch some TV and pretend to myself that nothing had happened. I had my lines to learn, and that would take my mind off it. I was calming down, beginning to feel better. Forget about it, I told myself, but if it gets worse, tell a teacher. I resolved to take my own advice.

Ten

I was running down a dark alley, wet bricks glistening either side of me. I had to move as fast as I could because someone or something was gaining on me. I could hear the footsteps. I realised my strength was running out. My legs felt as if they could hardly move. The thing was getting nearer. I tried to scream but my mouth made no sound. It was too late, and I clutched tightly on to the duvet...

I clutched tightly on to the duvet, damp with sweat, and wondered whether I really had cried out in my sleep. My heart was pounding in my chest. I knew I'd had a nightmare and although it was a relief to be awake and in my bedroom, the horror still clung to me. I got up and switched on the light, wanting everything around me to be as normal and bright as possible. It was quarter to three in the morning.

There were my school books on my desk, my poster of Jarvis Cocker on the wall, some clothes I should have hung up lying on my chair. Bit by bit, I was able to calm myself down. I would have liked someone's company, but it would have been a bit soft for an almost-sixteen-year-old to go and wake her mother. A nightmare was nothing special. I told myself it was only a dream and I should go back to sleep. I decided to think of something to help me relax. I reminded myself it was almost my birthday and I was going into town with Rachel to get something new to wear. I knew I wasn't to tire her out as she was still recuperating from her op, but she would be OK for a few hours. I wondered what I should look for in town – some new jeans, perhaps? Mine fitted well but were getting tatty. Would I be able to afford a new denim jacket, or should I get something a bit more glam? These were interesting questions, and trying to think of the answers helped me to drift back into a peaceful sleep.

I was very tired in the morning and found it hard to get up. What's more, Dad was in a temper and Mum was flying about the house looking for some essays she'd lost. I got out of bed at the last minute and skipped breakfast, trying not to think about what awaited me at school. Yesterday I had called Lisa a slag. It was make or break time. Either she'd call it a draw or be out for blood. Automatically I put on my blazer and checked I had enough money to see me through the day. For some reason I felt as if my life was happening to someone else – perhaps I was still spaced out from the sleep I missed last night.

Luckily Mum offered me a lift to school, and I

accepted gratefully. If there was going to be a showdown with Lisa, I preferred it to be in school rather than out.

On account of the lift, I was early. When I arrived in the form room only a couple of boys were there, playing cards. One of them had a small radio tuned to Radio One. I said hi, and they nodded.

I didn't need any books for the first lesson. We had PSE with Mr Weston, where we were supposed to discuss issues like drugs and personal safety, how to study and things like that. At Chillingham we'd had the same thing only we called it Lifeskills. I liked it – not just because it wasn't proper work, but because we had good discussions and it made you think about life. Only Mr Weston didn't take PSE too seriously. He moaned that we had more important things to get on with, like passing exams; and last week when we had a session on soft drugs, he said it was probably too late to tell us all of this, and a waste of time given that half of us still couldn't spell. Why do these people who have such a low opinion of teenagers end up teaching us?

To pass the time I decided to have a look at my lines again. I had quite a challenging scene in the play when I explain to the Inspector what happened at Millward's store, when I blame Eva Smith for laughing because I was in a bad mood. She gets the sack even though she did nothing wrong. I was deep into the script when Leanne and Jodie came in. At first I didn't notice them. By the time I did they were standing right over my desk.

'You're in trouble, you,' Leanne said.

'What have I done?'

'You called Lisa a slag.'

'But she – '

Leanne cut across my words. 'Big mistake. She's going to make your life *hell*.'

'She called me a slag too!' I said, attempting to defend myself.

'Yeah, but nobody badmouths Lisa and lives,' Leanne concluded.

'We're just warning you,' Jodie added.

Before I could say anything else they had gone. The words of the play swam before my eyes. How on earth could they accuse me of calling her names, when she bloody started it? The unfairness of it stung me. Perhaps I should try explaining everything to a teacher, but who? And what if Lisa's gang all made out I was the villain? Who would they believe? What if there wasn't one witness who was prepared to tell the truth?

What did Leanne mean, that Lisa would make my life hell? What else was she planning to do? Slowly I realised that she had done nothing very serious so far – she had called me names, campaigned a little against me, played a joke with a tampon. That was nothing to what she could do. I could see that if Lisa really hated someone, there were no limits. None whatsoever. I shivered and nervously flicked through the pages of the play, trying to make out that Leanne's threats hadn't bothered me. The classroom slowly filled up.

'I've been given these sheets on – what is this rubbish? – assertiveness training?!' Mr Weston's voice was incredulous. 'As if you lot needed that! You could all do with being a bit less assertive, if you ask me. The trouble with you lot is that you don't know how to learn, how to shut up and listen. The last thing I want is you laying down the law to me.' He stopped and read the headings from the sheet he was holding. '*Assertive, aggressive, passive, manipulative.* What a load of psychobabble! *How to cope in confrontations . . . how to cope with criticism . . . broken record . . .* I do not believe it! Right – take it from me – you can't learn about life from books. Now, since the senior management in its wisdom has decided that I have to have a record of exactly how each of you travels to school and which bus routes you use, as if I haven't got enough to do, what with them not bothering to cover the maternity leave properly, I propose to get this done now. Now that's what you call being assertive.'

I felt disappointed. I would have liked to learn something about assertiveness training. It sounded interesting, and useful, too. But the last thing I wanted to do now was draw attention to myself by asking if I could look at the material. I was trying to keep a low profile. I was intensely aware of Lisa and her gang at the back of the classroom, and although I could not see them, I imagined them following my every move, waiting for an opportunity to pounce.

Mr Weston called out our names one by one and we had to go up to his desk and give details of our travel arrangements. While he was doing that, some of the class were getting on with last night's homework, chatting or reading. I got out my maths exercise book and covered the words on the page of my playscript to test myself on my lines. Then I felt something sting the back of my neck. An insect? I rubbed it, and the stinging subsided.

Then there was another sharper sting. This time I looked immediately behind me. Lisa and her mates were deep in conversation, some other girls had their heads down, reading, and the boys were mostly looking out of the window. I pretended to carry on learning my lines but every nerve in my body was alert, waiting. Sure enough, there was another sting, then another, and something soft landed in my hair. I felt for it – it was a small, paper pellet. Angrily I looked round again. No eyes met mine but Claire was giggling. It was all the evidence I needed. As soon as the boy who was with Mr Weston returned to his seat I left mine and walked to the teacher's desk. It was a knee-jerk reaction. I'd had enough. And if Lisa's definition of 'making your life hell' consisted of flicking pellets, then she ought to be easy to deal with.

'Sir,' I said, 'someone's flicking pellets at me.'

'Right, who is it?' he asked, raising his voice but sounding rather weary.

Predictably, there was no reply.

'OK. Unless someone owns up you're all in detention. It's room 14 tonight. Mr Derby is officiating.'

'Oh sir!' whinged one of the boys. I felt embarrassed, as if the detention was my fault.

'Was it you, Owens?' Mr Weston remarked.

'Me, sir? I can't even aim straight.' The boys around him laughed. Feeling horribly conspicuous, I decided to go back to my place.

'It's your last chance,' Mr Weston told the class. Not a murmur, not a movement. It seemed as if they were all in league against me. 'Right,' he said. 'Anyone who doesn't turn up to detention tonight will do an extra week, as well as a fortnight on bin duty.' He resumed his work.

My face was burning. I had got the whole class in trouble when I knew it was only Lisa who was the culprit. Ought I to explain that to Mr Weston? Perhaps the time had come for me to let him know what had been going on. Another pellet grazed my neck. This time I pretended not to notice. I was summoning my courage to do what I knew I should have done ages ago – tell a teacher what was going on. I felt relief and fear in equal proportions. Relief that maybe someone would be able to stop the torment, and fear that I could be making things much worse.

At the end of the lesson I waited for the others to leave and I approached Mr Weston again. He was concentrating on the forms in front of him and barely acknowledged me. I felt as if he was my last resort.

'Can I have a word with you?' I asked.

'Now?' He glanced at his watch.

I didn't know what to say. I remained silent. There must have been something in the expression on my face that alerted him. He looked up from his papers and gestured for me to begin.

'Those pellets – I think I know who was responsible. It was Lisa Webb and her mates. They don't like me very much. They've been hassling me.' This was harder than I thought. It was difficult to find the right words.

'Lisa Webb? I'm not surprised. She's a bad lot. You're not the first to have had trouble with her, and you won't be the last.'

That didn't make me feel any better.

'Mind you, you're lucky it's only pellets. Girls are always worse – they're underhand. At least with lads they sort it out with a clean fight.'

'It's not just pellets,' I stuttered. 'She's been spreading rumours.'

87

He looked relieved. 'Spreading rumours? Sticks and stones may break your bones, but words can never harm you. Keep your chin up, Jac. It'll soon die down, once you've settled in. I tell you what. I'll let the rest of the class off detention, and I'll make sure she goes. Look – I've got to go now – it's my only free lesson of the day and I'm gasping for a coffee. Here's some advice: try to laugh it off. Show her you don't care. That's the best way to deal with that sort. Good girl for coming to tell me.' Already he was packing up his things and going.

I felt cheated. He hadn't taken me seriously at all. I could have been shouting alone in a soundproofed room for all the good it had done. I was old enough to know that sometimes teachers get it wrong, and Mr Weston had got me wrong. I thought over what he had said. Maybe once I also believed that you could laugh off bullying, or that you could pass off cruel comments. Not any more. I was scared.

The next lesson was maths, but I didn't feel as if I could face it. I wouldn't be able to concentrate. All I knew was that Lisa was out to get me, and Mr Weston wasn't going to do anything about it – in fact, by putting Lisa in detention on my word, he was making things infinitely worse. In my desperation I thought perhaps the best thing to do might be to apologise to Lisa – stupid, I know. I began to think that if I explained to her that I liked her, that I never meant to call her a slag, that I'd like to be her friend, she might change her attitude. But cold fear was constricting me like a snake, and I could hardly breathe. The reality was I had an enemy, and I didn't know what she was going to do next. Standing here in an empty classroom, I felt more vulnerable than ever.

Why it never occurred to me before I do not know. There was someone in Markfield who was there to deal with these sorts of problems, and who instinctively I knew I could trust – Mrs Thornton. I remembered her kind face on my first day, and that she'd said I was to find her if I had problems settling in. I hadn't seen her since because she didn't teach me for anything. There was a glimmer of light at the end of my dark tunnel. She would know what to do.

I recalled where the head of year's office was and made my way there as quickly as I could. I rapped on the door but there was no reply. I guessed she would be teaching. I debated for a moment whether to get her out of her lesson, and decided I would. I was irresistibly drawn by the thought of her sympathy, understanding and help. I made my way to the school office to find out where she was.

The office was just next door to the reception area. Inside, there were three women at work, one typing, another on the phone scribbling down notes, and another crouching by a filing cabinet.

'Excuse me,' I said, 'I'm looking for Mrs Thornton.'

The woman who was crouching straightened herself. 'Sorry, love. She's gone. She started her maternity leave a week ago.'

All I could think of to say was, 'Oh!'

'What do you want her for?' the secretary continued.

'Oh, nothing. It'll wait,' I muttered. I walked away from the hatch that opened into the office. Then I had a thought and turned back.

'Has someone taken over as head of year 11?'

'Yes,' the secretary replied. 'Mr Weston. Shall I see where he is?'

'No, no, it's all right.'

I was filled with leaden despair as I made my way over to maths. It seemed as if I was meant to get through this on my own. Now it was a matter of just surviving one day at a time. Lisa wasn't in my maths group, but she was in history, which was next. Somehow I didn't feel as if I could face her, not until I'd got something sorted out. I decided a visit to the school nurse might be in order.

Luckily the nurse was there in the sick room. I told her I was having bad period pains and I asked for a hot-water bottle and a chance to lie down. She was an elderly, motherly woman and I watched her as she scurried around, filling up the hot-water bottle. I wondered if I should tell her what had been going on, but I was feeling defeated, and tired too, and really only wanted to lie down and think about nothing. I clutched the hot-water bottle to my stomach and read the notices on the wall about head lice, healthy eating, the signs of meningitis and the consequences of German measles.

I felt numb, and I think I drifted off. Later a kid came in with a migraine, and that brought me to again. As I woke up I decided there and then to tell Rachel everything. I'd ask the nurse if I could go home, and that way I could avoid Lisa today. Today was Friday. Tomorrow was my birthday and my shopping expedition with Rachel. I'd be damned if I'd let thoughts of Lisa spoil that but, nevertheless, this time I really would speak to Rachel. Rachel would know what to do. She just had to.

Eleven

I woke after a long and dreamless sleep, and opened my eyes to realise it was my birthday. I decided I wouldn't give anything that had happened yesterday head space, until I had a chance to be alone with Rachel. Until then, I was going to enjoy myself. You only turn sixteen once.

Even though I wasn't a kid any more, my parents still did what they've always done on my birthday – got up early and put all my cards and presents out on the kitchen table. There were various things from relatives, some chocolates and a Body Shop gift set from Mum and Dad, and an envelope containing money for me to spend in town that afternoon. I gave both of them a big hug. I knew that money didn't come that easily these days.

Nor, for that matter, was it easy for my mother to let me go into town without her to buy clothes. She doesn't entirely trust me to spend large amounts of money – I should have thought that was the one thing she could trust me to do! When I was younger and she absolutely insisted on taking me shopping for clothes, it was hell. Every skirt I tried on was too short, all the 'in' colours were too lurid, and anything fashionable was overpriced. Then she would stand outside the changing room muttering 'hurry up, there are people waiting' and, worst of all, she'd open the curtains before I'd put on the clothes, and I'd be displayed in my bra and knickers for all the world to see. Or she'd wander over to another section of the shop to look for clothes for herself and wouldn't be around when I wanted to show her something.

So, as you can see, it was a present in itself just to go out for clothes without Mum! I said I'd take the bus in, although when I was standing at the stop it did occur to me that Lisa might show up or might be on the bus I caught. I stayed downstairs and quickly scanned the passengers. There was no one there I knew. I started breathing again. I determined once more to put her out of my mind and was surprised to discover what an effort of will it took. She said she would make my life hell, and she was doing it, though perhaps not in the way she'd intended. I wondered if she realised how much all of this was affecting me.

Rachel was being dropped off by her parents at the bus station, which served as a gentle reminder to me that I shouldn't tire her out. In fact, Rachel was already waiting for me at the bus station when I got off the 93. She handed me my present, and I asked her if I could open it straight-away. Inside, I discovered a beautiful silver necklace with a dolphin pendant. The card she gave me had a smiling face on the front with the command 'smile!' I did.

'Where d'you want to go?' Rachel asked.

'It's up to you. You mustn't get too tired.'

'Oh no, not you as well! I'm not an invalid just because I had my appendix out. My mother keeps fussing over me all the time. Anyway, it's great to see you.'

And it was great to see Rachel. She was dressed in jeans and a pink Benetton sweater. I thought she looked as if she'd lost weight, but I didn't want to say so in case that encouraged her to think it would be better to lose even more. Her blond hair was tucked behind her ears and she was wearing some frosted eyeshadow.

'I like your eyeshadow,' I commented.

'It was free with a magazine,' she explained, as we threaded our way through the crowds on the way to the shops. 'It's cool, isn't it?'

The shops were in a glass-covered shopping centre that calls itself a mall. All the chain stores are there – Dolcis, New Look, Etam, WH Smith and the rest. Recently they've built a coffee area in the middle of the central square, and you can get espressos and cappuccinos and home-baked cookies. It looks quite continental, if you really use your imagination. Today the mall was packed. I liked that; it gives me a buzz to see everyone's lives in motion. I always feel excited when I'm around lots of other people.

First, Rachel and I wandered into Penny's, an accessory shop. We fingered bangles and necklaces, examined earrings, body glitter and hair mascara, but felt a little bit old for all of that. The other girls in the shop looked about twelve.

'Come on,' Rachel said. 'We'll go somewhere else.' She pulled me by the arm. 'There's Our Price. Always full of blokes.' I let myself be led to Our Price and we made out we were reading the charts while quickly checking out the talent. There was no one very interesting there – mainly nerdy types, adding to their carefully catalogued CD collection. I realised that I was getting used to being with boys all day, and just standing in a record shop wasn't as much fun for me as it was for Rachel. I reminded her why we were in town.

'Shall we go and get me some trousers?'

'You're on,' she said.

We went into New Look and wandered through rails and rails of clothes. It was hot and noisy in there, with music playing loudly in the background. Rachel drew my attention to some black jeans, but they weren't really what I had in mind. I examined some black hipster bootlegs in a shiny material.

'What do you think of these?' I asked her.

'OK. Try them on.'

We made our way to the changing rooms at the back of the store. I quickly surveyed the crowd to see if Lisa was around. It had become a habit. The girl at the entrance to the changing area gave me a hard plastic tag to take in with me, and I found an empty cubicle. Quickly I slipped out of my jeans and put on the black trousers. They fitted low on my hips and exposed a good area of flesh below my midriff. They looked great. I knew my mother wouldn't like them, and that was a recommendation in itself. But what would Rachel think? I left the cubicle and made my way to the entrance.

'Rach? What d'you think?'

'Wow! You look . . . I've never seen you in trousers like that before. Are they really you?'

A good question. The answer was, they weren't really me, but they were the me I wanted to be.

'I like them,' I said to Rachel.

'They suit you,' said the assistant, who'd been listening to us. 'What you need to go with them is a little skimpy top.'

I agreed with her. With the trousers still on, I popped out of the changing area and looked through the sale rack, to find a ribbed top in powder blue. I tried it on, and the tightness of it emphasised my bust. The whole effect was amazing. I didn't know where I would wear the outfit, but maybe there would be some Christmas parties. I grimaced at myself. I wished my hair was longer and I was wearing more make-up. I twisted round to check the price labels and realised I could afford the whole outfit.

'I'm going to get them both,' I told Rachel, once I had changed back into my own clothes.

'Great,' she said, a shade noncommittally.

'You know what would go with this outfit?' I said, as we queued to buy it.

'What?'

'Getting my navel pierced.'

'What if it went septic?'

'It wouldn't if I kept it clean.'

I paid for the items. As we left the shop Rachel remarked, 'You've changed since you started at Markfield.'

'What do you mean?' I countered. Had she noticed anything?

'You wouldn't have mentioned about getting your navel pierced.'

'Yeah, well,' I said. Had I changed? The atmosphere at

Markfield was certainly different from Chillingham. The boys, and the fact the school wasn't selective, did count for a lot. Even without the business with Lisa, I'd have had to adapt. It was a bit like living in another country and picking up the language. You had to do that if you were going to survive. At the time I didn't realise this. I just felt a little prick of resentment at Rachel for commenting on my behaviour.

'Check out *that*!' Rachel said suddenly.

I looked ahead. There, in front of her, was Thornton's. Rachel was ogling the display in the window lasciviously. I joined her. Rachel loved chocolate. So did I, but not with the devotion Rachel showed. Chocolate was Rachel's religion. On impulse, I decided to spend the rest of my birthday money on both of us.

'Come on,' I said and pulled her in. We chose the chocolates we wanted from the display in the glass cabinet, and I watched her mouth water. We ate the chocolates walking through the precinct. All conversation stopped.

Fuelled by strawberry truffles we wandered into Bhs and had a quick look at the clothes there. Then we noticed they had a hat section. Rachel tried on a straw hat with flowers on the side, only it was far too big and it made me giggle. I found a navy straw hat with a floppy brim, pulled it down over my face and pouted seductively in the mirror, which had Rachel in stitches. We kept an eye out for the assistant but luckily no one was around.

Then Rachel found a black hat with a high crown and tried that on. It made her look like a chimney sweep. Then carefully I removed from the stand a cream hat with a silk ribbon round it and a veil, and put that on.

'We look like we're getting married,' Rachel said.

Still laughing, we moved over to the men's hats. Rach popped on a trilby, and I found one of those hats with earpieces that hang down, like Sherlock Holmes'. When I put that on she creased up. I looked at my reflection in the mirror and began to splutter. To my embarrassment I noticed someone was looking in the mirror with me and smiling too; someone familiar, with dark hair, heavily lidded eyes, eyes I was used to gazing into and imagining they belonged to my fiancé, Gerald Croft. Neil! I froze, and didn't even have the presence of mind to take the damn hat off.

'Hi!' he said. 'It suits you.'

Now I whisked it off, any poise I had draining from me rapidly. I looked helplessly at Rachel. She was puzzled. I realised I ought to introduce everyone.

'This is Rachel,' I explained to Neil.

'Hi, Rachel. How's your appendix?'

Rachel blushed furiously. Even her neck went pink.

'Mike? Look who's here!' Then Michael – Eric Birling – came strolling towards us. It was just as I'd imagined it, and yet horribly different: in British Home Stores, in the men's hat department, Rachel scarlet with embarrassment and me lost for words.

'What are you doing here?' Neil asked.

'Shopping. It's my birthday,' I said, collecting myself.

'Happy birthday, Sheila! We're going for a drink – why don't you come with us?'

'Where are you going?'

'To the coffee place in the square.'

'Shall we, Rach?'

She nodded.

As we all walked off together, I felt my knees

trembling. It was partly the shock of meeting Neil, partly the thrill of his invitation (was it a date? I would discuss the technicalities with Rachel later), and partly the effect that Neil always had on me. Also I was nervous, as this was the first time Rach had met Michael. Would she like him? Would she look at him for long enough to see whether she liked him?

None of us said anything until we reached the coffee area. Neil insisted on buying the drinks, as it was my birthday. I didn't think I could drink anything but asked for a diet Coke. So did Rachel. She was still silent, but I saw her smile at Michael, and he smiled back. Things were looking good. By that time, I'd recovered my composure and I'd begun to chat away, discussing the progress of the play. I even asked Neil what his plans were for next year, when he left Markfield. He wanted to take A Levels at the sixth-form college – chemistry, physics and maths.

I took very tiny sips at my Coke, but that was all I could manage. It was as if my stomach was guarded by a 'No Entry' sign, and I bitterly regretted eating all those chocolates.

'So how are you settling in at Markfield?' Neil asked me.

'Great,' I lied. 'The teachers are all right – for teachers.'

'Yeah,' he said. 'Who's your form teacher?'

'Mr Weston.'

Neil pulled a face. 'Hard luck. He can be a right bastard. Hey, I don't know many of the people in your class. Who do you hang out with?'

'Do we have to talk about school?' I joked. 'It's my birthday, after all.'

I quickly asked Neil what kind of music he liked listening to, then we got on to music in general and Rach and Michael joined in once or twice. Neil was so easy to talk to that I found I relaxed into the whole situation – even though I still fancied him like mad! A smile was playing around Rachel's lips and I guessed she was having a good time, too. While I didn't want the afternoon to end, I was almost wishing it would, so Rach and I could start reliving every minute. We were chatting about the play again, which meant Rachel was a little left out.

Michael asked her, 'Are you going to come and see us in the play, Rachel?'

'Yeah,' she said to her diet Coke.

'Cool,' he said to his.

I wondered whether in the short time I'd been at Markfield I'd become more confident with boys. I couldn't help but notice how Rachel was fighting her shyness. Unfortunately, Michael seemed rather shy, too.

Neil checked his watch. 'We'll have to push off now. We've fixed a lift back home at three.'

He and Michael got up to go, and we all said our goodbyes. Neil wished me a happy birthday once more, and Rachel and I watched the two of them disappear into the crowd. When we were sure they'd gone, we both started to talk at once.

'So what do you think?' I asked Rach.

'Now I can see what you've been up to at Markfield!'

'Rach – what do you think of Neil? Do you reckon he likes me?'

'Well, he must do, otherwise he wouldn't have suggested coming for a drink.'

'Yes, but does he *like* me?'

'I think so. It's hard to tell. You could be in with a chance there.'

'And Michael – do you like him?'

We were talking so quickly we were hardly giving each other enough time to answer.

'Yes – yes, I do. Did he like me?'

'Definitely.'

'Jac!'

'Rachel!'

We both gave one of those silly girlie shrieks, basically because we couldn't think of another way of expressing how we felt.

'Maybe we should have asked them out,' I reflected.

'I would have died of embarrassment.'

'But someone's going to have to make the first move.'

'Can't we just encourage them?'

'How? Telepathy?'

There was a twinkle in Rachel's eye.

'We could hire a van with a tannoy system!'

'Or send them a singing gorillagram.'

'We could drape posters over the motorway junction roundabout – '

We hooted with laughter, like two big kids. I hadn't enjoyed myself so much for ages. The café was crowded, and conscious that we'd finished our drinks and there were people waiting for tables, we got up and walked out of the precinct, towards the gardens opposite. We were still chatting about the boys, going over what they'd said, and analysing it all.

'I think I really like him,' Rachel said wistfully. 'You're lucky. At least you get to see Neil every day. When will I ever see Michael again?'

'We can arrange something.'

'I wish I went to Markfield.'

'I wish you did, too. I could do with a real friend.'

As I said that, I knew the moment had come. I shivered, even though it was suprisingly warm outside.

'Thanks,' Rachel said. 'Have you made many friends at school? You haven't said much about the girls. You've just gone on about Neil all the time. Not that I blame you.'

This was my cue. I knew I had to tell Rachel what had been going on. I was silent as I debated exactly how to go about explaining everything. We entered the gardens and saw an empty bench opposite a statue dotted with pigeon droppings. We sat down and I put my New Look bag on the bench by my side.

'I haven't actually made any friends at school,' I said, matter-of-factly. I waited for Rachel to reply. I had the crazy thought that if I told her how unpopular I was even she would go off me. It was pure paranoia. But that's how being bullied gets to you. I wanted to tell her, and yet dreaded doing so.

'Why haven't you made any friends? Are they all in cliques or something?'

'Well, yes. But...' I fingered the wooden slats of the bench, tracing a whorl in the wood with my thumb. 'It's more than that. No one likes me.'

'How do you know?'

'I know. Some of the girls have been calling me names – it's stupid really – either they say I'm stuck-up, or that I'm a slag. And they've been flicking pellets, and other stuff.'

'What other stuff?' Rachel's voice was low and serious.

'Spreading rumours about me, saying I pulled the

drama teacher. Then they put a used tampon in my
school bag – '

'Who is "they"?' Rachel asked. 'Is there a ringleader?'

'Her name's Lisa Webb. She's got it in for me – I wish
I knew why. That's the worst part. Like, if I'd upset her, I
would understand her behaviour, but I haven't done a
thing. Only I keep thinking I must have done *something*.'

'You haven't done anything. It's not your fault.'

'I know, but . . .'

'Have you told anyone?'

'I sort of spoke to my form teacher and he put Lisa in
detention. He said she'd stop after a time.'

'Oh, Jac!' Rachel looked horrified. She took my hand.
'That's dreadful. You shouldn't have to put up with all
those things. It's bullying. Why didn't you tell me before?'

To my surprise, I felt as if I wanted to cry. Despite the
meeting with Neil, despite the fact it was my birthday, I
was fighting to hold back the tears. I realised then that
nothing, nothing in the world feels as bad as being
disliked and rejected. Up until now, I'd been partially
denying what had been going on at Markfield. I'd even
been reluctant to call it bullying. Telling Rachel had made
it real. Then Rachel's pity brought out my self-pity.

'You were in hospital,' I reminded Rachel. 'I didn't
want to upset you.'

'But you must have been so miserable!'

I pushed her sympathy away. I was afraid of breaking
down in tears. 'Well, yes, but there was the play – and
Neil. And I think that in a way Mr Weston was right. The
girls are mean because they don't know me yet. It might
all settle down.'

Rachel said nothing.

'I was silly to think there wouldn't be trouble. I expect I seem different to them.'

'That doesn't give them an excuse to be horrible to you.'

'No, but it explains it. What if I made more of an effort to be like them? Even if I'm just pretending, maybe they'll stop harassing me. What do you think?'

'I think you should tell your parents.'

'Come on! You know my mum – she'd go ballistic, and they'd insist on going into school, and it'd be worse than ever.' In a funny way, I felt Lisa was stronger than my mother. I couldn't imagine my parents' intervention achieving anything.

'Well, if you don't want to tell your parents, speak to another teacher.'

'I don't know them yet.' I thought of Mr Jennings, who I did know, but I couldn't possibly speak to him, not after the rumours about me and him. That way was barred.

'Then go and find a youth counsellor,' Rachel persisted. 'We can go together to the library. There's bound to be a leaflet there. Or ring Childline.'

'I'd feel a fraud. My problem isn't serious enough. I'm not pregnant or a drug addict.'

'Oh Jac – you know it's not like that. If you won't do anything about it, I will. What about contacting Kidscape? They tackle bullying.'

'Kidscape? I'm not a kid!'

'Forget the name – bullying is bullying, whatever age you are. I'm going to write to them for you. Then we'll find out what to do.'

I was cornered. I couldn't stop Rachel writing. I was

grateful to her for taking the issue out of my hands.

'All right,' I said.

'Don't sound so grateful!'

'I am – but I just don't want the whole thing to escalate. Like, what if Neil finds out about what's been going on? That'll really make him fall for me, knowing I'm being bullied. I still feel I should be able to deal with it by myself. I don't want them to be punished – I just want it to stop. That's all.'

'By getting advice we can work out how to stop it.'

'Do you reckon?'

'I do. Hey, you've got me now,' she said affectionately.

My eyes filled with tears, but I refused to cry. I couldn't begin to tell Rach how much she meant to me, ever. Although the situation hadn't changed, sharing it with Rachel had been an immense relief. I felt as if I wasn't alone any more, or as if I'd been carrying a burden that was far too heavy for me, and Rachel had come along and taken some of it, and now it was easier for me to keep going. I wished I could do something to show her how grateful I was.

Should I buy her another box of chocolates? A whole shop of chocolates wouldn't be enough to show her how I felt. So instead I just squeezed her hand.

Twelve

All in all, it was a good weekend. Not only did I feel better about things at school, but Dad had secured a big order on Saturday afternoon, which meant business was beginning to look up. Dad said he thought we might eventually be better off than ever before; Mum affectionately called him an unreconstructed optimist, and remarked that I took after him. We all hugged each other. For a little space of time I forgot about Markfield.

But the truth was my own problems pressed in on me like an evil face squashed and flattened against a window pane, leering, trying to get in. Sometimes I'd forget about Lisa and Markfield, then suddenly I'd remember, and the fear and misery seemed worse than ever. I was tense, not at all myself, and my parents had commented once or twice that I didn't seem as lively as usual. I passed it off as a combination of having a lot of work and boy-problems.

I think my parents were relieved to hear that, and they didn't push me any further.

Sunday night was bad – I've never liked Sundays, the way school looms in the distance. Now I dreaded it. I was apprehensive about seeing Lisa, but on the way to school on Monday I tried to convince myself that the weekend might have made her forget her threats. In fact, she didn't turn up to registration, and my mood lightened as I imagined she was away. No such luck. I glimpsed her in the art room; she'd only been late.

She entered the classroom sullenly for the afternoon register. She glanced at me, but if anything her eyes looked sad, I thought. I wondered if she had trouble at home. Perhaps bullying me had just been a phase. She went and sat at the back of the classroom among her friends. I was still alone. Although I'd suffered no open hostility today, no one was being friendly.

At quarter to four I went along to the drama studio for my rehearsal, to find a notice pinned to the door. Mr Jennings had had to go to the dentist and the rehearsal was cancelled. I felt disappointed. I was looking forward to seeing Neil again, believing that our relationship had come on considerably over the weekend. Feeling a little let down, I made my way to the school library, thinking I'd use my free time to get something interesting to read, and some books for my history coursework. We were doing something on the build-up to the Second World War.

I found what I was looking for, and ended up leaving school about half an hour later than I would otherwise. To my annoyance, as I approached the bus stop, I saw my bus moving away. Even if I ran, there was no way I could catch it. Now I had a choice. I could either wait another twenty minutes for the next one, or walk round the corner and catch the 91, and change to pick up the 93.

I couldn't be bothered to wait for twenty minutes, and so I decided to get the 91. As I turned the corner there was the bus, and I ran as fast as I could, determined not to miss that one, too. As I got to it, the doors were just closing, but the driver saw me and let me on. It was full downstairs and so I went upstairs, saw some seats near the front, made my way to one and found I was sitting next to Leanne. My heart skipped a beat.

'Hi,' I said, thinking it best to acknowledge her.

I took my bearings. All four girls were there, Leanne, Jodie, Claire and Lisa, each of them taking up a whole double seat. Lisa and Jodie were smoking. They all looked at me as if I was something the cat had dragged in. I wanted to run, but I was conscious of how humiliating that would be. I decided to sit tight. Behind me there were a few kids from school and some adults, so they couldn't do anything too dreadful. The bus heaved and shuddered as it moved off down the road, past the Fiat garage and Do It All.

Lisa left her seat and came and sat with Jodie, so she was in front of me. She turned round and smiled.

'Want a fag?'

'No thanks,' I said.

'Shame. You'd find it relaxing.' Then she blew smoke straight in my face. It stung my nose and made my eyes water. Lisa offered a cigarette to Claire and Leanne, and they both took one. Soon I was surrounded by a fog of cigarette smoke. A woman behind us shouted that we weren't supposed to smoke on the bus. Lisa answered her

with a couple of words that left her tutting and complaining to the other women she was with. The girls
laughed. Then Lisa pushed her carton of cigarettes into
my blazer pocket.

Leanne announced loudly, 'It's her who's got the
ciggies. She gave them to us.'

Jodie choked with laughter. I took the cigarettes out of
my pocket and gave them back to Lisa.

'No.' She refused them. 'Try one.' It sounded like a
dare. For one reckless moment I considered taking one.
But I'd seen pictures of lungs blackened by cigarette
smoke and I knew the dangers. I wasn't about to risk my
health just for Lisa's friendship.

'No, thanks,' I said again.

'Too effing posh for a fag,' Lisa intoned, mimicking
what she thought was my accent.

'Snob,' called Jodie.

'I'm not a snob,' I said, desperately. 'You've got me
completely wrong. Just because I went to Chillingham
doesn't mean I'm any different from you. I can't help it if
my parents sent me there. I left because my dad lost his
job, and we're quite hard up.' My voice sounded thin and
reedy, but I couldn't pass up this chance to put the record
straight. 'If I seem stuck-up, I'm sorry. I don't think I'm
better than anyone else – I've probably got a lot in
common with you. Just give me a chance, OK?'

'Just give me a chance,' whined Leanne, trying to
imitate me, as she blew smoke in my face and flicked ash
on my skirt.

'Shut it, Lee,' Lisa said. 'You heard what she said.'

Leanne looked surprised.

'Yeah,' Claire echoed. 'She said she wanted to be friends.'

I looked at all four girls, and watched them consult Lisa with their eyes. She remained serene, stubbed out her cigarette, took the lipgloss from her pocket and began to apply it. We were all silent, waiting.

She said to me, 'You can hang around with us, if you like.'

'But Lisa, you said – '

'Cut it, Jodie. I've changed my mind. Jac's all right.'

Those were words I never thought I'd hear. My gamble had worked – Lisa had finally accepted me. Or so it seemed then. More than anything I wanted to believe what she had said and be taken into their charmed circle. Imagine how invulnerable I'd feel, as one of them. I said goodbye to my common sense, blinded by the glory of having friends again, and what friends! And if I had to change myself a bit to fit in, well, I could do that. I couldn't wait to tell Rachel what had happened. Maybe she hadn't posted that letter to Kidscape yet. I could stop her.

Lisa smiled at me, and I smiled straight back. 'Friends?' she questioned.

'Friends,' I said. Then I saw the Frogmore Arms junction, where I had to change. 'I've got to get off now – see ya tomorrow.'

'Bye,' Lisa said, and Leanne, Jodie and Claire echoed her. As I walked down the bus, I received a filthy look from the two women, but I didn't care. I was 'in' now, and life was bearable once again. I thought things could only get better.

The following day, I sat next to them all in registration, and at lunchtime it was taken for granted that I was going to the chippy with them. It was obvious that everyone in the class had noticed my changed status. Lisa's approval was like a passport to a better land. A couple of boys said hi to me and some girls asked for my answers to the maths homework.

After we'd had our chips, we followed Lisa to a place she knew where we could go for a smoke. I followed her to the alley behind the shops, where black wheelie bins stood in a line and rubbish littered the tussocky grass. We sat alongside each other on the brick wall. The sound of a radio floated down from a window above the rear of a shop and the sweet smell of rotting fruit and vegetables laced the air. In the distance we could hear traffic roaring by on the main street.

'We're going to the Lemon Tree on Friday night,' Lisa said. 'You coming?'

The question was addressed to me.

'The Lemon Tree? What happens there?'

'They have a club night for fourteens to sixteens once a month. There's no alcohol but you can get tanked up beforehand.'

'A club night,' I said, playing for time.

'Yeah. Dancing and stuff. And pulling lads.'

Claire giggled.

'Well,' said Lisa, sounding just a little impatient, 'you coming?'

I felt at a loss. Normally I'd have asked a little more about the club, but there was no way I was going to lose the ground I'd gained with Lisa. The idea of meeting lads was appealing, too – both Rachel and I had agreed that our social life needed a kick-start. And if she came too, and I could wear my new outfit...

'What time's it start?' I asked casually.

'The doors open at eight,' Claire said. 'Oh, come on, it'll be a laugh.'

'Will your mum and dad give you permission?' Leanne asked. I thought I noticed some sarcasm in her voice, and that decided me.

'If I want to go, I'll go,' I replied.

'So are you?' Lisa said. I felt I was being pushed out on a precipice again. I felt strangely hesitant. My better instinct told me I should have backed out there and then, that I was getting myself in too deep, but still I was terrified of losing their friendship. I was quiet while they went on about the club night.

'Last month Lisa pulled fifteen boys,' Claire went on. 'We counted. And Leanne went round the back with the DJ after.'

'He thought I was seventeen,' Leanne said. 'He didn't half have a shock when I told him how old I was. He reckoned he'd be in trouble with the law.'

Jodie shrieked. 'What the hell were you doing with him?'

'Never you mind!'

They were all laughing, sharing in some secret that excluded me. Leanne whispered something to Jodie that made her laugh, and then told Claire, too.

Claire said, 'I think that is so sick!'

My imagination was running riot. I felt a little frightened again, and hoped that by going to the Lemon Tree I wouldn't be out of my depth. It was true I'd never been to that sort of thing before, and in that respect I was a little behind everyone else. It was time I caught up. Besides, I would only do what I wanted to do. How babyish I was, imagining the Lemon Tree as full of drug-crazed ravers having sex on the dance floor! It was time

I grew up and got myself a life.

'What shall I wear?' I asked Lisa.

She smiled lazily at me. 'Anything. Skirts, hipsters, whatever. Only no jeans.'

'OK,' I said.

Lisa's eyes held mine for a moment. Her look puzzled me. She seemed satisfied, as if she'd got what she wanted. Even then, I didn't hear the alarm bells ringing.

'I'm going to get my ear pierced,' Jodie said, breaking the silence.

'But it is already,' I observed.

'No, higher up, so I can wear a chain.'

'I'll do it for you, if you like,' Lisa said.

'Can you . . . Can you pierce ears?' I asked.

'Yeah. I've got a needle in my pocket.' She brought it out. 'You can use a compass point but it's a bit thick.' She bent over Jodie, who was laughing and screaming.

'No, I didn't mean it, Lisa. Oh all right. It'll save me a few quid. Ow! Stop it! Help! No, I've changed my mind! Oh, God! It's bleeding!'

She pushed Lisa away and put her hand to her ear. I watched, horrified and fascinated. As she took her hand away I saw a droplet of blood growing, shining like a ruby, and then it plopped onto her shoulder.

'You cow, Lisa!'

Lisa laughed, her eyes glittering with amusement. 'You're soft, you. Look, I'm going to give myself a tattoo.'

I watched her as she began to prick the needle into the skin on the back of her hand, each prick drawing blood. She was biting her bottom lip, intent on what she was doing. Again and again she jabbed her hand. I saw the letter 'L' form itself.

'Doesn't it hurt?' I asked.

There was no reply. When Lisa had finished, she looked up, triumphant. Then she made a fist of her hand and slowly lifted it to me, so I could see the letters.

'What do you think of that?'

Her fist was directly in front of my eyes. For one fleeting moment I thought she was going to hit me. I almost flinched.

'It's cool,' I said.

Lisa laughed, and the tension broke. I was glad I was her friend now – she was the last person you'd want as an enemy.

I slipped up on my lines a couple of times in the rehearsal that night. Mr Jennings joked about it. The truth was, I wasn't concentrating on my acting. I was wondering whether to change my mind about the Lemon Tree. When I had been with Lisa and her gang at lunchtime I had decided to go. There was no way I was going to risk my new-found popularity. Anything, absolutely anything was better than being isolated like I'd been before. Then during history, when Mrs Sugden was talking about Neville Chamberlain and the Munich agreement, I'd got cold feet. I reckoned that Lisa, Leanne and everyone would know lots of people at the Lemon Tree, and they'd ignore me. Or they'd all pull and I wouldn't. I didn't fancy being left high and dry in a place I didn't know. I could take Rachel with me, of course. Yet I recoiled at that idea. I could always spin some story to Lisa about how I'd forgotten we were going away that weekend, and wriggle out of it that way. But on the other hand, what could happen that was so bad at an arts centre in the middle of our town? If the worst came to the worst, I would just ring Mum and Dad and get them to collect me.

Because of chatting to Claire, I was late for the rehearsal, and didn't have a chance to talk to Neil. He was already on the stage when I got there. I began to wonder whether he would be at the Lemon Tree. It was a distinct possibility. Once again, I decided I ought to go. And then for the life of me I couldn't remember the next words Sheila Birling was supposed to speak, and I dried up. Neil looked sympathetically at me.

'OK, folks, we'll take the scene from the beginning.'

I could have kicked myself for not concentrating, and soldiered on.

Later, Neil and I were watching Eric Birling with the Inspector when the drama studio doors opened and the art teacher came in.

'I've finished them, Pete,' she said.

'Great!' Mr Jennings turned his attention from the stage and Michael and the Inspector stopped. 'Excuse me a minute,' he said. 'That's Miss Garwood, head of art. She's doing the set.'

The two teachers were soon involved in complex discussions about stage furniture, slats, partitions and lighting, which left the cast free to chat.

'It was ace meeting you and Rachel on Saturday,' Neil said.

'Yeah!'

'Did you have a good birthday?'

'Brilliant.'

'Did you and Rachel go on some – '

The Inspector, a tall and rather imposing year 11 boy who obviously knew Neil, interrupted our conversation.

He gave me a curious glance.

'Friend of yours?' he asked Neil, indicating me. His voice was a little suggestive.

'Jac's a good mate,' Neil replied.

Michael joined us, followed by the boy playing Mr Birling, a chubby Asian boy who was in my maths group. He had a beautiful speaking voice. When all the lads were together, they started fooling around, laughing about a mistake Michael had made in one of his lines, and exaggerating it. I laughed too, feeling as if I were an honorary member of the boys' group. The other girls at the rehearsal, and there were only two of them, hung back. I had a grin fixed to my face as I listened to them. Neil was no longer paying me any attention at all; it was as if I didn't exist. I felt badly let down.

'Men!' I exclaimed to Rachel on the phone that night.

'But he said you were a good mate,' she reminded me.

'That's what he'd say about another guy. It's what he'd say about Michael. I'm sure he doesn't fancy me.'

'Yes, but you don't *know*. And boys behave differently in groups to when they're alone.'

'I'm not getting my hopes up.'

'And is Lisa still being nice to you?'

'Yeah, she is. And Rachel, she's asked me to go with her and the others to a club night at the Lemon Tree. Do you want to come?'

'A club night?'

I explained to her what Lisa had told me and elaborated a bit. 'Dancing, techno music, that sort of thing.'

'Oh, I don't know! It's not my scene – and I don't have anything to wear.'

'Oh, go on!' I tried to persuade her, but to be honest, my heart wasn't in it. Somehow I couldn't imagine Rachel with Lisa, Leanne and co. My instinct was to keep them apart.

'Are you going to go, Jac?'

'I might,' I said. 'I'm thinking about it.'

I thought about it as I lay in bed that night, trying and failing to get to sleep. I was curious to see what a club night was like, and then there was the question of Neil. Today he'd treated me as if I were one of the lads. I could see I needed to change my behaviour. A night out with Lisa and her gang might teach me a thing or two. I recalled scenes from my favourite musical, *Grease*, when Sandra Dee transforms herself into a vamp and gets Danny. What if Neil was at the Lemon Tree and saw me looking fantastic?

Now here was a good getting-to-sleep fantasy. I planned it all down to the last detail, me in my hipsters and skimpy top, smoochy music playing, Neil looking at me as if he'd never really seen me before, and as we leave the club together he opens his umbrella to protect me from the rain and puts his arm around me.

Thirteen

I was right about the rain. It drummed relentlessly against my bedroom window as I put on my make-up, and there was even a distant rumble of thunder. This was a major hassle, as it meant Dad would insist on driving me to the Lemon Tree. I was supposed to be meeting Lisa, Leanne, Jodie and Claire just outside and the last thing I wanted was Dad leaning over to kiss me goodbye as I got out of the car.

I went downstairs to the living-room.

'Goodness, Jac! You're exposing nearly all of your stomach!'

'They're hipsters,' I explained to my mother.

'And the top's a bit tight. I hadn't realised you'd grown so much.'

Don't you just hate it when you're standing in front of your parents hoping they'll say you look fantastic and all they do is criticise? I'd spent hours in the bathroom trying to get my hair to stay in place, and a few more hours getting my eyeliner straight.

'You look lovely, Jac,' my father said.

I grinned at him. At least one parent knew how I felt.

'I suppose you do look quite nice,' Mum added. 'It's just that these fashions... There's a tendency these days for girls to dress like floozies just because it's fashionable. I read an article in the paper about the effect of Barbie dolls on the generation – '

I left Mum to her sociology lecture and went to the hall to get my denim jacket. I refused to let her upset me because I knew she was under pressure at work again, and that was why she was carping at me and Dad at the moment. But Dad was in a good mood, and I could rely on him to cheer her up. He stood up, got the car keys out of his pocket and winked at me.

'Are we off then?'

I insisted Dad drop me round the corner. We agreed to compromise on the umbrella, however, and I approached the Lemon Tree with Mum's floral retractable umbrella protecting me from the rain. Outside the arts centre was a large man in his thirties in a puffa jacket – a bouncer, I suppose – and some people of my age, boys mainly, fooling around. One or two of them had their heads shaved, and they were dressed in sports gear. The girls who were with them were huddled in a bedraggled group. There was no sign of Lisa and the others. I wished I hadn't dismissed my father so readily.

I went over to the entrance and there, to my relief, I saw Leanne. She and Lisa were standing just inside the

118

foyer. There were a couple of lads with them.

'It's Jac!' shrieked Leanne. She was wearing a tiny denim skirt and a tight black T-shirt. There was glitter on her face.

'Hi, Jac,' Lisa said. 'This is Steve and Tony.'

I looked briefly at the boys. One was tall, gangly and had bad acne. The other had bleached hair and smirked. Lisa looked a lot older than she did in school. She wore a short black dress and her legs were bare. Her hair was tied up at the back with a butterfly clip and her lipstick was bright red. She smiled at me as if she was genuinely pleased to see me. Her eyes lingered on me, but so much I felt just a shade uncomfortable.

'Where's Jodie and Claire?' I asked.

'They've gone in already. They're in the bog. Claire's not well. Come on.'

Lisa left the boys behind and we three moved off towards the table where they took the tickets. I went into a cloakroom area to get rid of my dripping umbrella and jacket, then followed Lisa and Leanne into the main hall.

The music was pretty loud and the repetitive rhythms seemed to make the floor shake. It took my eyes some time to adjust to the dim lighting and for me to get my bearings. At one end of the hall were the DJs with their equipment. There were quite a few people around, mainly standing in groups. I checked to see what people were wearing and as far as I could see I was the only one in hipsters, which made me feel conspicuous. I surveyed the boys hoping to see Neil but there was no sign of him. I guessed he might turn up later.

Lisa and Leanne were standing a little way away from me, whispering something. I watched some lads dancing, if you could call it dancing. They were going beserk, punching the air to the rhythm of the music. None of the girls were looking at them but just standing around in tight groups. I was beginning to feel a bit nervous.

In fact I now had a suspicion that the evening might turn out to be terminally boring. Since Lisa and Leanne were ignoring me, I decided to check out Jodie and Claire.

'I'm going to the loo,' I told Lisa.

'Yer what?' She hadn't heard what I'd said.

'I'M GOING TO THE LOO!' I repeated.

I left the hall and made my way there. I found Claire immediately. She was sitting on a chair looking vague.

'Hi,' I said. 'Are you all right?'

'Jodie's throwing up,' she said. Her speech was slightly slurred. Some rather unpleasant sounds were coming from the end cubicle.

'What's wrong?' I asked.

'It's the vodka,' Claire said. 'Oh, God!' She put her hand to her mouth and ran towards the cubicles. They were all full. She threw up in the sink. I turned so as not to see her. Then she turned the taps on full and at the same time Jodie emerged.

'I feel better now,' she said. 'Oh, look, it's Jac. Hello, Jac. Glad you could come, Jac.'

Her sarcasm wasn't lost on me and I wondered what had brought it on. I felt uneasy, but I supposed she was still drunk. Meanwhile, Claire wiped her mouth on the towel roll that had come loose from its holder and re-adjusted the clips in her hair. Jodie put on some more lipstick. They were dressed almost identically in satin-effect blouses and black micro-skirts.

They both put an arm through mine and we went back to the main hall.

The music seemed louder than ever and now there was a psychedelic light show playing on one wall. I could feel the beat of the music reverberate through my body, but it wasn't my kind of thing. I strained my eyes for Lisa and Leanne and finally spotted them. Each of them had their arms wrapped round a lad, kissing them. Then one of the boys I'd been introduced to earlier approached Claire.

'D'you wanna go with me?'

She did. He grabbed her and the next thing I knew, Jodie had gone with a boy too and I was all alone.

It was what I'd feared – being left marooned like this. I felt foolish. I should never have come to the Lemon Tree tonight. Wrong people, wrong place. This wasn't my scene at all. I knew now that my idea that Neil might turn up was daft, too. This wasn't his kind of place, either. Nor Rachel's. Nor Michael's. I began to feel smaller and smaller, as if I was watching everything through the wrong end of a telescope. I knew for certain that I shouldn't have come. Everyone was pairing off for a quick snog, and although I would have quite liked to be asked, the last thing I wanted to do was go with some complete stranger. But it is always nice to be asked...

Feeling out of it, I decided to get a drink from the bar, which was at another end of the hall. I saw some girls I knew from Chillingham but they either didn't recognise me or didn't want to. I got a bottle of diet Coke and sipped at it from time to time, feeling bereft. As much as I knew this place wasn't me, that all-too-familiar feeling returned of being an outcast, a reject, an oddity. I felt my adult self dissolving, and the child in me demanding that

I go home. If only I'd insisted Rachel had come with me. This wasn't a good place to be alone, and I felt vulnerable and upset; anxious that all my so-called friends had deserted me.

At that low point, Lisa reappeared.

'Hey, Jac!' she shouted. 'I've got someone here who wants to meet you!'

She came up to me with the boy with bleached hair in tow, the one that had gone with Claire earlier. He was smirking more than ever.

'Hi,' I said, and got up. Big mistake. He took my hand and pulled me onto the dance floor.

'What's your name?' I asked. I couldn't remember if he was Steve or Tony.

He didn't answer. He just jerked me round and started kissing me. I was too surprised to do anything about it. He tried to open my mouth with his tongue but I kept it firmly shut. He pressed his body against mine as hard as he could, kissing me until I couldn't breathe. His hot hands were on the bare skin above my hipsters. There was no way I could struggle free. After what seemed like an eternity, he broke away from me.

Lisa and Leanne had been watching.

'Well done, Jac! Hey Jodie! Jac's been with Tony.'

Jodie and Claire came over then, followed by the gangly acne-ridden boy. I saw him look directly at my top, then he put an arm around my waist.

'Push off,' I said.

He laughed, ignored me, and before I could do anything about it he was kissing me, too. His mouth was wet and slimy and his hand moved around my back, going lower and cupping my bum. It was awful. I remembered

his acne and squirmed as he pressed his face against mine.
I couldn't tell him to go away as it was impossible to talk.
I knew if I opened my mouth his tongue would be in it. I
struggled but he was bigger than me.

'Look at her go,' someone screamed.

I fought like fury. Eventually he gave up. When he did,
I could swear I heard applause.

'Jac, Jac,' Leanne was chanting.

I swivelled round. There was Lisa, Leanne, Jodie, Claire
and some other girls from school, all in a circle, clapping
in time to the music. I was in the middle, piggy in the
middle. Another boy was introduced into the centre of
the circle. He looked scruffy and older than me.

'Go for her, Dez!'

Briefly I saw his shaven head and piggy eyes. He
grabbed me and my attempts to fight him off were futile.
He was even stronger than the others, and more determined. He kissed me sloppily, but was more intent on
feeling me – his hands were everywhere. When he
grabbed hold of my breasts I heard cheers and whistles.
Lisa's voice rose above the cacophony.

'He's got her tits!'

I was terrified. I tried to rip his hands away from me
but he acted like it was a game and as I removed one
hand he put another elsewhere. Everyone was still
clapping and cheering. He smelt of sour alcohol,
cigarettes and sweat. When he tried to thrust his hand
down the front of my hipsters I slapped him round the
face, hard. There was a peal of laughter from the
spectators.

I was wild with fear. I honestly thought he was going
to rape me, there, in front of everyone, and all of them

123

were willing it to happen. The fear gave me a strength I never knew I had and I finally struggled free from my attacker and tried to break out of the circle of onlookers. They stood close together, deliberately blocking my passage. I had to fight to separate them. As I did, I felt a sharp kick on my shin. That was Lisa. I pushed against Claire, and she gave way. Lisa tried to stop me, and held me by the arm, pinching me tight. She looked directly into my eyes. I shall never forget what I saw there. Her eyes were alight with excitement, even pleasure. They smiled at me almost caressingly.

'Slag,' she said. 'Bloody effing slag. Did you like your little surprise?'

Then she spat in my face.

I ran out of the hall, rubbing my cheek furiously, too shocked to cry. The foyer was full of people. I would have run out of the building and gone straight home but it was late, it was dark, and I was terrified. Instead I made for the pay phone in the corner and rang home. I prayed someone would answer quickly. Pick up the phone, pick up the phone, I begged silently.

There was no reply.

Where on earth could my parents be? I didn't think they'd had any plans to go out. I'd told them to pick me up at half past ten, and now it was half past nine. It was possible they'd gone for a drink in town – that was Dad's favourite method of cheering Mum up. I was completely marooned.

The phone rang and rang and I hoped against hope there would be a reply. Then out of the corner of my eye I saw the last boy who'd assaulted me. I put the phone straight down and ran to the loo.

Once there, I splashed cold water on my face and caught sight of myself in the mirror. My face was red, my hair dishevelled, my eyes wild with fear. I felt disgusted with myself and wanted more than anything to wash and scrub those awful feelings from my body. But the Ladies was a mess. There was a girl sitting on the chair with her head between her legs, her friend looking on anxiously. There was a puddle in a corner. The towel was now festooned all over the place and tissues littered the floor. A gaggle of suspiciously young girls were putting on make-up at the mirrors.

I didn't want to stay there, but outside was worse. That guy was outside and, worse than that, Lisa was outside, Now there was no saying what she would do to me. It was hard to accept that she had planned all of this, that the friendship she'd offered me was just a trap. I was so stupid; all the signs were there, but in my desperation I had wilfully blinded myself. She had been playing with me like a spider with her fly. The truth was she hated me, hated me so viciously that she was prepared to plot and plan to make me suffer. My pain was her pleasure.

Liquid fear shot through me, but also a conviction that there must be something dreadfully wrong with me, for me to attract hatred like that. Even those boys – they didn't fancy me – they'd mauled me as if I wasn't even a person.

The girl on the chair slumped down and passed out. Her friend screamed.

I left the Ladies, looking around to check that the boy had gone, while one of the bouncers went in to try to help the unconscious girl.

That gave me an idea. Close to me stood another one of the bouncers, a strapping bloke in a puffa jacket that made him look twice his size. There was something about the expression on his face that made me feel I could trust him.

'Can I wait with you for my parents?' I asked. 'I'm not having a very good time and I don't want to go back inside.'

'Sure thing,' he said. 'You stay here with me.'

I did, for what was left of the evening. After twenty minutes or so Lisa came out of the main hall, with Leanne and two more boys. She saw me and smiled.

'Hi, Jac. See you at school on Monday. I'll be waiting for you.'

'Friend of yours?' enquired the bouncer.

'No,' I said. 'She hates me.'

The bouncer furrowed his brow. 'That ain't good.'

'I know.'

'Perhaps she's jealous,' he said. 'A nice-looking girl like you.'

He didn't say that in a flirtatious or suggestive way. He was just thoroughly nice. His kindness saved me. He chatted to me on and off, and showed me a picture of his baby daughter, her hair tied prettily in little knots. Talking to him got me through the rest of the evening, and helped me keep my composure when finally I saw our car draw up outside the Lemon Tree. I thanked him warmly and walked down the steps to meet my parents.

I didn't say much when I got in the car. I told them that I hadn't had a very good time, that it wasn't really my scene. They said they'd thought as much, but it was as well that I'd tried it and found out from experience. Once we got home I said I was exhausted, and went straight to bed.

★

Of course I didn't sleep. First I hid under the duvet and sobbed. I didn't want my parents to hear me. If they did, I would have to explain what had gone on, and I wasn't prepared to do that. I couldn't bear to relive it – I wanted to forget everything that had happened, deny it all. But of course, that was impossible.

Once when I was little and had been playing in the garden I'd found a dead bird that had been savaged by a cat. I ran away screaming, but then I kept going back, to take a look, as much as I could bear, then I ran away again, then came back, until I was able to look at it without flinching. In the same way, I revisited what had happened that night. I shuddered as I recalled what the boys had done, but most of all I trembled as I thought of Lisa, and the expression in her eyes.

What had I done to deserve being treated like that? This was what I couldn't understand. It was the randomness of it, the terror of realising I could inspire such hatred, when up till now I'd thought of myself as lovable. My universe rocked slightly. Lisa made me see myself in a new way, made me loathe myself, as she loathed me.

At the same time, I knew I wasn't loathsome. My rational mind told me that there was nothing wrong with me, but that there was something wrong with Lisa. Yet she was the one who was popular, and I was a reject. Perhaps there was something wrong with the whole world, then. I cried some more, burying my face in the duvet.

I'd never intentionally done anything to hurt some-one. Lisa was different to me. It clearly gave her pleasure to hurt me. Why? That was what I couldn't understand. How could hurting someone give you pleasure? I tried to imagine being Lisa, being in that circle that had laughed at me tonight, and I wondered what she'd been feeling. Was she glad that her plan had worked? Did she feel powerful? Perhaps that was it – she wanted power. When people were scared of her, she felt she could control them. Perhaps there were people who wanted to feel power like that. I'd read enough in magazines to know that bullies have often been bullied themselves or have a lot of problems at home. But I couldn't bring myself to feel sorry for Lisa, not after what she'd done to me tonight. Even if she had problems, that was no excuse for taking it out on other people.

I lay on my back now, my eyes wide open, staring at the ceiling. I could just about make out the shape of the light shade. It was chilly in the bedroom. Gusts of wind howled outside, rattling the window panes.

I couldn't remember ever feeling as frightened as this. I'd had nightmares before, but when I'd woken up, they'd dispersed, become nothing. Now my nightmare was reality. Yet sleep, and dreams, would not come. Lisa hated me, and I was powerless to stop that hatred.

I began to wonder what would happen next. 'See you at school on Monday. I'll be waiting for you.' Those were ominous words. Yet she couldn't do anything that dreadful inside school, under the eye of the teachers. Where I needed to be careful was out of school. I'd better make sure I didn't travel alone. It might be an idea to alert Rachel to what had happened, just the outline, not the details. Best to forget all about those.

Once I was happy, full of hopes, dreams, ambitions. Now life was going to be about survival only.

I tried to think about Neil. Would he get to know

about what had happened tonight? Gossip travels fast, and I couldn't imagine him not finding out. Then he would go off me entirely. That thought was dreadful, unbearable. Whether he became my boyfriend or not, I didn't want to lose his friendship. He was the only good thing that had happened to me at Markfield. I wanted to keep him separate in my mind from the sordid, frightening reality of my life. He was the only dream left to me.

When I tried to conjure up his face again, it became all mixed up with the horrible lads who'd imposed themselves on me. So I stopped thinking about Neil.

I still couldn't sleep. The wind outside had dropped, and now I could hear the rush of blood in my ears, and wondered if I could cause my heart to stop beating, simply by willing it to do so. I knew I couldn't. I knew that life went on, even if you didn't want it to.

That, really, I was powerless.

Fourteen

On Saturday Mum wanted to go shopping in town for a suit. During the next week she was going to be interviewed for a new job – in fact it was her old job, but there was some sort of reorganisation going on in the college. It was why she'd been so stressed recently. The plan was that I would go with her.

In the morning I explained to her that I thought I was coming down with something, or I was premenstrual – either way, I wasn't up to going out. She was disappointed, but didn't push me. She made me take some Paracetamol and extra vitamins. I stayed in, and it was lucky I did because while Mum was out, Rachel called round. I wasn't expecting her.

'It's you!' I said, surprised.

'Yes, it's me! Mum dropped me off and she's picking me up in a couple of hours. She had to call in at Gran's.

Look. I've got the stuff from Kidscape.'

She had with her a large brown envelope and began to take leaflets out of it. I felt myself flinch inwardly. I knew I needed help but seemed reluctant to take it – I thought admitting it was some sort of defeat. Rachel, however, was excited. Whenever she's involved in a plan or scheme, she talks nineteen to the dozen.

'Look! It's brilliant. There's a booklet here on how to beat bullying, and another one called "Stop Bullying". I've read them all. It explains about what makes people bullies, and how you can develop assertiveness to put them off. But most of all it says you've got to tell an adult. Here it says – look! – "you do not deserve this" – that's so true. No one deserves to be bullied. And you should keep a diary and write down everything that happens to you. Schools ought to have an anti-bullying code, and if there isn't one, parents can help to get one implemented. And – '

'Shut up, Rachel!' The way she was bubbling over with good ideas seemed utterly irrelevant to the hell-hole of misery I was in. To her, my problem seemed as easy to solve as a question in a maths test. Not only that, but she seemed to be taking over my situation. She was doling out advice in ladlefuls. I didn't want her to do that – I wanted her to sympathise with me. I needed her to hear how wretched I felt. Only she wasn't giving me space to talk. So I clammed up entirely and then I made her shut up. She looked at me rather mournfully. I felt remorseful and knew it was time to tell her what had happened yesterday.

'Actually, last night didn't go too well. Some things happened.'

'What things?'

My mouth was dry; the words wouldn't come. I took a deep breath in order to collect myself. Then I tried again, and suddenly found I was crying, with great gulping sobs. Rachel looked on, horrified. She hugged me while I cried uncontrollably, then fussed around me, Rachel-like, putting on the kettle, making me a cup of tea with far too much sugar in it, and settling me down. Bit by bit, I told her everything.

She listened, dumbstruck. 'Oh, Jac! It must have been awful!'

I tried to smile. I wanted to be brave.

'I'm so sorry for you.' She was quiet then. Once again I experienced that wonderful sense of relief I felt whenever I shared my problems with Rachel. We were silent for a while.

'Jac, you're going to have to do something now. You know that.'

I shrugged.

'Read these booklets, for a start. I'll leave them with you.'

I didn't reach out to take them. My limbs were heavy and aching. Perhaps I was coming down with something. My head was muzzy and I felt listless and apathetic.

'There's some good advice in them,' Rachel persisted. 'Tell an adult what's happening to you.'

'Not yet,' I said. 'Soon.'

'OK. And another thing. They suggest you ought to ring up or speak to the weakest member of the bullying group, and say how you feel. From what you've told me, I'd have a word with Claire. Ask her why Lisa is bullying you. She doesn't sound quite as bad as the others.'

I lifted my eyes and looked briefly at Rachel. It was easy for her to have these good ideas; she wasn't suffering like me.

'Please do something, Jac. It's changing you. You're all quiet. I want the old Jac back.'

I didn't want to tell her that the old Jac was killed off last night. I left her on the dance floor. So I decided to act a bit.

'I'm OK really. I suppose I'm a bit tired; I didn't sleep too well last night. And everyone's tense in this house because of Mum's interview. That's why I can't really talk to her about all this.' I chatted about Mum's job problems for a while.

'Have you seen Neil at all?' Rachel asked.

'I'm going off him,' I lied.

Rachel's eyebrows rose.

'I'm not in the mood for talking about boys,' I said. 'I think I must be premenstrual. I'm sure I'll be back to normal soon. I'll read those booklets, and, yeah, I'll probably have a word with Mum or Dad. Why don't we think about some nice things now? I'll show you what Mum and Dad got me from the Body Shop, and then we can watch a video.'

'Are you sure?'

She looked at me, full of concern. I couldn't meet her eyes. It was almost impossible to fool Rachel.

'Come on, I feel loads better.' I tried to sound as cheerful as I possibly could. 'Let's go up to my room and I'll give you a face mask.'

After Rachel left, I spent the rest of Saturday watching TV, curled up on the sofa. On Sunday I did my homework in the morning and lazed around all afternoon, feeling increasingly jittery as the day went on. It occurred to me that I needn't go to school on Monday at all if I carried on my pretence of being ill.

All Sunday afternoon I debated what to do. The idea of just staying at home indefinitely was so tempting. If only it were that simple. If I shammed illness, Mum would insist on taking me to the doctor, and she would be certain to suss me out. If I didn't go to school on Monday, I'd miss the lunchtime rehearsal, and I didn't want to let the rest of the cast down. In the end, I'd have to go back to school, and whenever that would be, I'd have to face Lisa.

I slept in fits and starts all through Sunday night, and I was in a deep sleep when my alarm went off on Monday morning. It jolted me awake. I could hear someone in the bathroom and birds arguing outside my window. Automatically I washed and dressed, declining breakfast, saying that it was too early to eat. Mum was reading a pamphlet called 'Your Interview and How to Succeed'. Dad was poring over some figures.

'Can someone run me in to school today?' I asked. 'I've got to be in early.'

My parents glanced at each other, and it was my father who agreed to take me. In a few minutes I was sitting beside him in the front seat of the car, and he was turning out of the drive. Suddenly the temptation to tell him everything overcame me. It would be so easy. In the privacy of the car I could give him an outline of events, then ask him to turn round and take me home. He would ring up school, and the nightmare would be over. I took a deep breath.

'Bloody hell, Jac! Did you see that? He was trying to cut me up.' My father gave a two-fingered signal to a driver, who gave one back. Dad's always been short-tempered at the wheel, and it was my fear he'd get himself involved in one of those road-rage situations. I told him to calm down, and then he went on and on about people who shouldn't be in charge of cars. The moment had passed. It was no longer the right time to talk to him. Perhaps later, I thought.

Lisa wasn't in registration; she was late again. All I had to put up with was everyone's reaction as I walked into the classroom. It was obvious that gossip about Friday night was all over the place. As I went to sit down, several conversations around me stopped abruptly. I heard muted laughter and noticed grinning faces. Doing my best to ignore everyone, I pretended to read. The back of my neck pricked with shame. It's a devastating feeling, being the object of ridicule. I couldn't concentrate on my book; instead I tried counting backwards, just to keep my composure.

At that point Jodie and Claire walked in. I glanced up at them and I saw, I thought, in Claire's eyes, something like embarrassment. I remembered what Rachel had suggested and, although at the time I'd scoffed at her, I now wondered whether it was worth speaking to Claire.

Shortly afterwards Mr Weston came in, his shirt not tucked properly into his trousers. He took the register quickly and I prepared to go to history. Claire did history too, and Jodie didn't. It was a golden opportunity.

I fell into step with her as I walked along the corridor.

'What you did to me on Friday night was really mean,' I said.

She was silent.

'Why did you do it?'

'It was Lisa's idea.' Claire couldn't look me in the eye. I was encouraged.

'Why did you join in?'

'It's hard not to, if it's Lisa.' She was quiet again. Then as we walked along, she mumbled, 'I'm sorry. I didn't think it would be as horrible as that. I thought it would only be one boy.'

I didn't respond. This was a hard conversation for both of us.

'What have I done to upset Lisa?' I asked.

'Nothing. I suppose we all thought you were a bit weird in the beginning, but then Lisa just had it in for you. She had it in for me in the second year for a time. She wrote these notes, slagging me off. Then, I don't know how it happened, but we became mates. You have to, really. Look, I'll be your friend, but keep it quiet. And if I were you, I'd stay right away from Lisa. I know she's planning something else.'

We reached the history room. I went to sit near the front as usual and Claire went to the back to join Cassie.

So Claire was scared of Lisa, too. That was interesting, and it was good in a way to feel I wasn't the only victim. Yet with that crumb of comfort had come more bad news. Lisa was planning something else. I didn't want to think what that could be. At least I had an ally now, although a weak one. I knew Claire would do nothing to jeopardise her position of safety. But she could warn me, and her solidarity had succeeded in making me feel just a little better. Then I smiled to myself. As usual, Rachel had been right. I was pleased I'd spoken to Claire. I would have to swallow my pride and tell Rachel what had happened. I resolved that when I got home that night I'd look at those leaflets she'd left.

Because I felt slightly more alive now, I actually paid attention in the history lesson. We were doing the causes of the Second World War and had been looking at events in Germany in the 1930s, like the rise of the Nazis and all the changing allegiances in Europe. It was all quite interesting. Then the discussion stopped and the teacher began to explain our coursework to us. We had to do a project on the Jews in Germany, anti-Semitism and the Holocaust. She handed out a book list and gave us a deadline. Thinking about all of this took my mind off Lisa.

In maths, which was just before break, I asked the teacher if I could be excused. I wanted to go to the toilet now, not at break, in case Lisa was around then. The teacher didn't mind. At break, I went to the staff room and stood around outside. Lots of people were there asking to see teachers, who were coming out at intervals to hear excuses about homework and requests for help. I reckoned I was safe there.

At the end of break I saw Lisa. She was coming towards me with Leanne. Our eyes met, and it felt as if there was only me and her in the universe. She advanced towards me.

'Say anything about Friday night and you're dead.'

I just looked away. I thought she sounded pathetic.

'Jac,' she called. 'I've got something to show you.' Unwillingly I turned in her direction. Something glinted in her hand. I think it was a Swiss Army knife. She pressed on it and a blade jerked out.

'Cool, isn't it?' she said, then closed it, and put it in her pocket. She and Leanne walked off down the corridor.

My first reaction was to think that they were just posing, and that they wouldn't dare use a knife. Then I remembered Lisa stabbing herself with the needle, and her clenched fist in my face. I wasn't so sure after all. She was perfectly capable of violence. And you didn't need to be strong to use a knife, you just had to get up close to your victim. I was ice cold with fear.

I believed then that I was facing certain danger. I was the fox, and the hounds were gaining on me. The mental torture I was in was as agonising as the physical pain I was anticipating. Would she really go as far as using that knife? My rational self kept telling me she wouldn't dare, but I couldn't control my thoughts. Where would she slash me? I wondered. My heart was palpitating and my stomach was clenched tight. The bell rang to signal the next lesson.

At lunchtime I went straight to the drama studio to try to eat my sandwiches. It was no use; I felt sick to the pit of my stomach. After five minutes Mr Jennings came along with a couple of the cast members. Neil walked in shortly after. As soon as I saw him, the attraction I felt for him flared up again, but it hurt me. The time in the coffee place in town seemed so long ago. I wondered whether he'd found out about the events of Friday night. I stole a glance at him, and thought he seemed a little distant.

Luckily, all we were doing today was a walk-through, an entrance and exits practice. I wasn't capable of real acting. I was fully preoccupied with working out how I could get home from school without meeting Lisa. Just making sure I wasn't alone would not be enough. It would only take a moment for her to slide that blade into my skin. Or maybe she would just threaten me with it, and tell me to do something humiliating. My mind was dark with lurid imaginings. I didn't see then that I was doing Lisa's work for her, thoroughly frightening myself. I didn't realise that for most bullies, the threat of violence is enough to get them what they want. I felt the danger was real, and maybe it was.

At all costs, I had to avoid her. She was bound to be watching me all the time. If I left school early, she would leave school early. If I lingered, she would linger. Mum and Dad were both at work and out of reach.

Even in my state of total panic, I noticed that Neil looked lovely today. He'd washed his hair and the sunlight coming in through the window made it shine. His shirt was crisp and white. He smelt gorgeous. I noticed that whenever he looked at me he seemed embarrassed, and more and more I became convinced he'd heard something about Friday night. My shame was complete. At the end of the rehearsal Mr Jennings talked about our costumes. I didn't listen. I went to get my bag as the bell went for registration.

At that moment Neil approached me.

'Hi,' he said.

'Hi.'

'Look, I know this might sound a bit strange, but you know your friend Rachel?'

'Yeah?'

'Can I have her phone number?'

'Sure, sure.' I recited it; I knew it off by heart.

'Cool. Thanks. See ya, Jac.'

I was stunned. How could I have been so daft? It

wasn't me he liked at all, it was Rachel. So would anyone; she was kind, ever so pretty, by far the nicer of the two of us. One meeting, and he'd been smitten. And I had been such a fool, dreaming about him, going on about him, when he fancied my best friend. I was stupid, stupid, stupid. I was so glad that I'd said to Rachel on Saturday that I'd gone off him. If she did want to go out with him, the field was clear. I didn't want to stand in her way.

Now the huge emptiness in my life seemed bigger than ever. It dragged at me, and threatened to suck me down into it. Slowly I made my way back to the form room. I almost didn't care if Lisa was there or not.

She wasn't. As I walked into the room I brushed past a few of the boys.

'Hey,' one of them said. 'What've you done to Lisa? She's out for your blood.'

I didn't reply but went to my seat. The English language teacher entered then, and five minutes later, Lisa followed.

'Sorry, Miss,' she said to the teacher. 'I've got a message for Jac. Can I give it to her?' She dropped an envelope onto my desk. There was nothing written on the front. Its whiteness glared blankly at me. I didn't have the courage to open it.

Instead I lifted my eyes and tried to concentrate on what the teacher was saying.

'. . . in different situations. I know some of you prefer working together and that's fine. But for those of you who want to have a go, you can give a talk to the rest of the class. It can be about a hobby or interest, or something you feel strongly about. A few years ago a student brought in a piece of music and explained what it meant to her, and she had us all in tears. Someone else spoke about her holiday in Majorca. Anything, as long as you remember to narrate clearly, speak up, and remember it's necessary to keep your audience interested. That's what good public speaking is all about.'

'Does it count for our GCSE, Miss?' someone asked.

'Oh, yes. I'm keeping records for all of you.'

I liked Miss Unsworth. She was always so enthusiastic and I thought she was a good teacher. Once I would have been the first to volunteer to give a talk. Not now. Not with Lisa in the audience, watching me.

'Who's interested?' the teacher asked.

A couple of hands went up. I felt Lisa's eyes on me. I looked down at the desk and saw the blank envelope. It mesmerised me. I was desperate to open it, but knew I shouldn't.

'On Thursday, then. All of you have a think before then, and whoever's managed to prepare something can have a go. If no one comes up with anything, we'll do some group work. But now I want to go over last week's comprehension.'

People opened their files. Ought I to read the note? I didn't want to; I knew that whatever would be in there would be bad. Not reading it was worse; my imagination was already running ahead of the truth. Clumsily I tore open the envelope. The note, to my surprise, was typed on a school computer. It wasn't signed. For a moment I thought it really was something official.

Hello f★★★-face. Enjoy yourself on Friday? Did it turn you on? If you think that was exciting, that's nothing to what's going to happen next. And don't think you can escape – no one escapes. Fat arse. Nobody here likes you, so piss off out of it, when we've finished with you. We've not finished with you yet, cow. I know where you live. You turd, you – '

And there was more. Worse insults, more expletives than I could have dreamed of. Just reading the note made me feel sick. And all this torrent of abuse was directed at me. *Sticks and stones may break my bones, but words...*

I shivered, as if in a fever. I tried to tune in to the teacher again but it was impossible. 'No one escapes... we've not finished with you yet'. What was she planning? She was planning something, something far, far worse than Friday night. My stomach turned over and for a moment I thought I was going to be sick.

Should I show Miss Unsworth the note? There was no absolute proof it was Lisa. She could always claim someone gave it to her to give to me. It was typed and unsigned. I could see stretching ahead of me a whole process of accusations and denials. Lisa was clever, and that made it a whole lot worse.

I forced myself to look at the comprehension passage. The words swam in front of my eyes. I felt dizzy – was my vision going? Scared I was going to pass out, I began to breathe quickly, and then I had a dreadful feeling that my breathing was going to stop. Nausea swept through me, and I put up my hand to be excused. I thought I was going to be sick right there in the classroom, in front of everyone. I managed to blurt out to the teacher that I didn't feel well, saw her look of concern, rose to go, and heard her say, will someone go with Jac?

'I will, Miss,' said Lisa. 'I'll go with her.'

I went rigid with terror.

'It's all right,' I mumbled. I sat down again.

'Are you sure you're all right?' Miss Unsworth asked.

I nodded, unable to speak. I tried to take deep, calming breaths, as my mother had taught me to do when she'd taken up yoga for a while. It seemed to help. I still felt cold all over. I hid the note in my file and began to think again how I could get out of school safely.

Inspired by fear, I came on a solution. I quickly checked my purse. Thank goodness it was Monday. Mum had given me money for the whole week. When the bell finally went I ran as quickly as I could to the school office. I explained that I didn't feel well, and that the nurse said I could ring for a taxi to take me home. They looked surprised, but let me use the phone. I asked if I could wait in the office until the taxi came. When it did, I ran out of school and jumped in the back, giving my address as I did so.

For a moment I felt elated. I had outsmarted my pursuers. Then I remembered the note. 'I know where you live.' Maybe that was just a bluff. I sincerely hoped so. I sat back, inhaling the smell of stale tobacco and petrol fumes. I was safe, but only temporarily. There was the problem of what to do tomorrow. There was no way I was going back to school. I knew I ought to tell my parents, but now I seriously doubted their ability to stop Lisa. Simply telling my parents didn't seem enough. And then they would be distraught that I hadn't told them earlier. No; the main thing now was just to keep myself safe and give myself some breathing space.

The taxi careered along the high street, weaving in and

out of the parked lorries and pedestrians, and I listened to the ebb and flow of instructions over the radio. 'Pick up in Market Street, anyone in the area?' My mother's interview was on Thursday, and she was manic with nerves. If she didn't get this position then she would effectively be demoted, she'd explained. Or even lose her job entirely, as her contract only extended to the end of the year. If only I could keep my problems to myself until Thursday. Surely I could survive until then.

I began to plan. I would be ill and not go into school until Thursday. I would stay at home and bolt the doors. I tried to think of an illness that lasted three days that didn't require a visit to the doctor. Maybe I should make myself sick and pretend I had a stomach bug. Planning like this helped take my mind off the threat hanging over me.

Before I knew it we'd arrived at my front door and I was paying the driver. I got the key from my purse and let myself in, as Mum and Dad were at work. I locked the door from the inside and bolted it, then my legs gave way, and I collapsed onto the floor and sobbed and sobbed.

Fifteen

It was easy to fool my parents. I just told them I was red-eyed because I'd had a headache at school, then I was sick and, worried I'd be sick again, took a taxi home. They told me I was very sensible and of course I could have tomorrow off. Mum was fussing a lot and blamed herself. I know she did, because I overheard her talking to my Aunty Jane, saying she wondered whether the stress she was under hadn't taken its toll on me. It was a convenient fiction.

I changed into my nightclothes and brought my duvet downstairs and snuggled under it to watch TV from the sofa. I liked that; I felt young again, protected. Only I was rather hungry and asking for something to eat would give the game away. I stayed up as late as I could and read for ages in bed. I refused to allow myself to think at all.

Since I fell asleep late, I woke up late, after Mum and

Dad had left for work. They had left me a little note saying they hoped I felt better, and with orders to contact them if I didn't. Since the coast was clear, I made my way immediately to the kitchen and assembled breakfast. I prepared toast and jam, poured myself a huge bowl of muesli and brewed some strong coffee. I switched on the TV again and tried to concentrate on some morning chat show. Then the phone rang. I panicked that it might be Lisa, but it was only Mum, checking to see if I was all right. Even then I couldn't see that with all this worrying, I was falling right into the trap Lisa had laid for me. She wanted me to worry. If I stopped worrying, I'd no longer be in her power.

The morning passed in a haze. I mostly watched TV but sometimes stopped, just to stare into the garden and gaze at the magpies hopping about importantly. I looked at the trees and wondered how old they were. It was odd to think that trees lasted longer than human beings did. Odd, and scary. It made me feel uncomfortably insignificant. Then I thought how it would be good to be a tree, and just exist without movement, without effort.

At lunchtime I went back into the kitchen to make a sandwich and see if there were any crisps. I assembled a plateful of food and took it back to the living-room. I was just about to tuck in when I heard the noise I had been dreading all day. There was someone banging on the door, determined to get in. She knew my address after all. I froze.

'Jac! Jac!' my mother shouted through the letterbox. 'You've bolted the door!'

I'd put the bolt across as soon as I'd got up, just in case. Now I hurried to the door and unlocked it to let my mother in. She was hyped up with nervous energy and wittered on at me.

'You shouldn't have put the bolt on, but I suppose you felt safer like that. Quite sensible, really. Ah! You've made yourself lunch!' She had spotted my dinner. 'Well, that's a relief. I was going to ring up the doctor's and take you to the emergency clinic, but if you're eating again you can go back to school tomorrow. Do you know, I thought you were coming down with something – you haven't been yourself lately.'

I realised she was oblivious to my mental state – she'd put everything down to a physical illness. I suppose that was easier for her to handle.

'I'm glad you'll be out of the way tomorrow because Maisie – you remember Maisie, she's a school governor – she's coming round to give me a mock interview. It wouldn't be much fun for you – you'd have to stay in your room. You're better off at school. Do you know what my head of department said today?'

She carried on dishing the latest gossip, while the sandwich I was eating turned to ash in my mouth. Her words had just sunk in; I would have to go to school tomorrow. Please God, I prayed, help me.

'You still look pale, you know, Jac, but it's best you go in. We don't want you missing all that work.'

I nodded. I picked up my bag and made for the door.

'Would you like me to run you in?' my father asked.

'No, no!' I said, quickly. 'I'm meeting someone on the bus.'

My parents smiled at each other.

'Bye,' I called, and went out. I walked to the bus stop,

then carried on. I had no intention of going into school at all. I'd never played truant before, but could see now it was dead easy. In my bag I'd stashed some jeans and a sweater, intending to find somewhere to change into them. Then no one would know I ought to be at school. I walked on until I reached Grove Road, where I knew I could catch the 85 straight into town, avoiding Markfield entirely.

I arrived at the bus station shortly after nine. I made straight for the Ladies. Some years ago, a woman was murdered there and I'd never used them since, but now I didn't care. I locked myself in a cubicle and changed my clothes. I waited for a while, then flushed the toilet so no one would suspect anything.

By quarter past nine I was back on the street.

What should I do? I had a whole day to kill. I thought I could pass some time by getting a coffee, and I wondered if the coffee place in the mall was open yet. I walked there and saw that already a few people were sitting around with drinks. I bought myself a cappuccino, took it to an empty table, the same table I'd sat at just a few weeks ago with Rachel, Michael and Neil. The contrast was unbearable.

Never had I felt more alone. The wrongness of not being in school made the whole world seem out of joint, and everything unreal. I knew I shouldn't be where I was. It was also odd thinking that no one at all knew I was here. Jac the outcast. I couldn't help but relate to Eva Smith, the victim in my play, *An Inspector Calls*. She was an outcast too, used by the Birlings before they spat her out. Unable to cope, she killed herself. It was her only way out. She chose an ugly, painful way to die and I shuddered as I thought of it.

If I committed suicide, I wouldn't do it that way. It would hurt too much. I'd try to choose a gentle method, if there was one. I'd heard that it was peaceful to drown yourself, but where I lived was miles from the coast. I knew a girl at Chillingham who took an overdose of Paracetamol. She was rushed to hospital to have her stomach pumped. People said she didn't really mean to kill herself, that her attempted suicide was just a cry for help. They said she was under too much pressure to do well at school.

I wondered what happened if you overdosed on Paracetamol? Taking the tablets wouldn't hurt, obviously. Then if you fell asleep and didn't wake up, everything would be over. Either you would be dead, or you'd wake up in hospital – either way, your problems would be at an end. Boots' was over the way. I was sure I had enough money for some Paracetamol.

The bliss of not doing anything, not being able to do anything, and being completely and totally safe...

Then I imagined my parents finding me after my overdose, and I thought about how they would feel, how horrified they would be, how they would blame themselves for the rest of their lives – no, I couldn't do it to them. There was no escape.

I finished my coffee and glanced briefly at the people around me. No one had noticed me at all. No one realised I shouldn't be there. I could have been a ghost.

I couldn't manage another coffee, but I didn't fancy wandering around the shops. There was also the horrific possibility that Lisa was playing truant, too, and I would accidentally meet her. Was there anywhere safe I could go? Then I thought of the Central Library. I could go there. I would just look like a student, and I could sit down in the warm, be comfortable and just read. Best of all, the librarians would be around. I would be completely safe. I lifted up my bag and left, my mind made up.

I crossed the road so I wouldn't have to walk past the Lemon Tree. The memories were still too raw. The library was open, and gladly I climbed the steps and walked inside.

It was a large library, with the librarians' station in the centre. There were racks of magazines, videos and CDs for loan, and row upon row of books. Fiction to escape into, reference books packed full of knowledge, craft books, cookery books, textbooks – then I remembered I had the history teacher's reading list in my bag, and I thought I might as well do some work on my assignment. I had a whole day to fill, and it was important to keep busy.

I found the history section, and there were several books on Germany in the 1930s. I selected one, took it over to a table and began to read.

I knew about the Holocaust, of course, and that Hitler didn't like Jews. It was interesting to read about the reasons why. Some of the Germans blamed the Jews because they lost the First World War, which is crazy when you read that 12,000 Jews died on the battlefield fighting for Germany. And Germany blamed them for inflation and unemployment. Then there was a lot of prejudice around – people thought the Jews killed Christ and had some sort of world conspiracy going. None of it was true. I knew that. It was weird and frightening that a whole country could be brought to believe these insane things, when any sensible person knew they were a pack of lies.

I just didn't understand that. There were some Jewish girls at Chillingham and they were exactly like the rest of us. It was awful to think that some members of their families might have been tortured or killed by the Nazis. I read about one night in which nearly 200 synagogues were burnt to the ground, and 20,000 Jews were taken to concentration camps, for no other crime than being who they were.

As I turned page after page, I became increasingly uncomfortable. OK, I could just about accept that the Germans were hoodwinked by Hitler, but what about the rest of the world? Why didn't anybody do anything? Were they frightened, too, or did they just not care? I read that there were fascists – a kind of Nazi – in Britain, too. I also read about people who tried to save Jews, only there weren't enough of them.

Then I came to a chapter about the concentration camps. I learned how trainloads of men, women and children would arrive there and be taken to buildings where, almost without warning, they would be gassed. Elsewhere, unthinkable medical experiments were performed without anaesthetic. In these camps, human bodies were processed into soap. I was stunned. I tried to imagine this happening to six million people, not just Jews, but anyone who was considered an outcast by the Nazis. I couldn't fit all this into my head. I couldn't understand how this could have been allowed to go on.

Then I turned another page. There were pictures. A photograph of a pile of human bones. Children and teenagers, my age, in striped suits, standing behind barbed wire. And then a photograph of a woman and her daughters getting off a train, walking to the concentration camp.

Because that picture was not as unspeakably awful as the others, I looked at it for a while. I couldn't imagine the death of six million, but I could imagine the death of this mother and her daughters. They could be my mother, me, and Rachel. How would I feel in that situation? Would I know what was awaiting me? Would I have a vain and silly hope that in that low, distant building I would be taken care of? Or perhaps I knew. I knew that something sordid, ugly and violent lurked there. That I would meet my death, falling to the floor in a gas chamber with hordes of other terrified people. We would call for help, but our calls would fall on unhearing ears; our torments would be witnessed by eyes blind with inhumanity. My last sight would be cold metal and dying bodies; my last breath would be contaminated by the stench of mass fear. And this happened more than six million times.

I sat with the book open in front of me. I wanted to be able to think that if I was alive then, I would have protested. Life didn't have any meaning unless it was to stop suffering, and to show people they were loved.

I remembered that just half an hour ago I was thinking of suicide. All over Europe people fought for their lives, fled for their lives, and there was I, ready to throw mine away. Life is the most precious thing there is, and I had been contemplating destroying mine.

For a moment I felt so small, so squashed, when I compared my own predicament to that of the Jews caught in the Holocaust. All my distress was over nothing, some fifteen-year-old kid with a taste for cruelty. I was the lucky one. How dare I make such a fuss!

Maybe that Jewish girl in the picture thought like that when the order came for her family to be taken to the camp. Better not make a fuss, better just go along with it. Maybe England thought that German anti-Semitism would just blow over, or that Hitler was a fool, not someone to be taken seriously. That was wrong. Inhumanity must be taken very seriously indeed.

I wasn't the only one Lisa had bullied. Claire had suffered, too, and probably numerous others. If I did nothing, there would be new victims. Bullies don't just grow out of it. The more they get away with, the more they can do. They live off fear and grow strong on it. That same poisonous fear had paralysed me, Lisa's victim. Only I didn't feel paralysed any more.

Sitting in the library, motionless, my mind ticking over, something happened and I stopped feeling sorry for myself. I'd realised that real strength comes from knowing when you need help and not being afraid to get it. I had a surge of energy, and deep inside felt the presence of the girl I had imagined, who lost her life through mindless brutality. I wasn't going to hide any more, or keep the bullying secret, as if in some way it was my fault. It was as much my fault as the Holocaust was the Jews' fault. It was time to do something; time to speak out.

Sixteen

I spent the rest of the day in a fever. I had the germ of an idea and it pressed on me, preventing me from concentrating on anything else, or even resting. I left the library and tried to relax by walking around town, looking in shop windows. I bought some food, which I ate on a bench close to the spot where I first told Rachel about Lisa. Some pigeons came strutting inquisitively towards me and I threw them a few crumbs from my egg sandwich. They stabbed and pecked at them as if they were in a tremendous hurry. They made me smile.

In the afternoon I returned to the library and looked up some more books on the list. Part of my idea had to do with collecting as much information about the Holocaust as I could. It was peaceful in the library, and when I'd finished I looked at some magazines, flicking through the fashions and the problem pages.

When I reckoned I could return home, I did my journey in reverse. I got back into my uniform still possessed by the sense that I could make things change. But how? That was what I wasn't sure of. I took the bus back home and noticed Mum's car on its own in the drive. At least the woman who had visited her was gone.

'Had a good day, dear?' my mother asked.

'Yeah, not bad,' I said.

'Good. Maisie came round,' she told me, eager to speak. 'She gave me a gruelling interview. I have to admit I'm a bit shaky on some of the management parts, but naturally I'm sound on subject-related questions. Oh, Jac – I forgot to ask. How is your stomach?'

'Lots better,' I said, opening the fridge to see what was in it.

'Good. Anyway, I showed Maisie the suit I bought and she said it was fine. But I can't get over it, Jac – being interviewed for your own job! As if they didn't know I could do it. Valerie, my department head, is behind it all, I'm sure. She's always sniping at me. I think it's jealousy – I'm more highly qualified than she is. That's why she's always given me the toughest groups. She'd love to see me kicked out. Not that she's that popular. But her husband plays golf with the principal and – '

Mum's witterings provided comfortable background music to my thoughts. I'd heard all this stuff about her college politics time and time again. I never really understood why Mum had put up with it all for so long. She chattered away, I half listened, then I gravitated towards the television.

It was only when I'd had supper and was up in my room, thinking about having a bath, when the idea suddenly took shape. I knew exactly what it was I had to do, and it was so simple I couldn't see why I hadn't thought of it before. Putting aside all plans for a bath I went to my bag, got out my jotter and a couple of the books I'd taken out of the library, and began to make notes. I covered page after page. I didn't notice time pass, nor the jabbering of the television set downstairs. When I had finished I read what I had written and began to cut it, changing it around, using my highlighter pens and thinking carefully about my delivery. I once thought Sheila Birling was going to be my finest hour. Not any more.

I woke up promptly in the morning, my mind sharp as a razor, adrenalin coursing through me. I hadn't forgotten it was my mother's interview (how could I? How could anyone?) and I hugged her and wished her good luck. I told her I had a good feeling about the day, and not to get too stressed out. I took my usual bus to school, saw a girl I recognised from my history group and chatted to her for a while about this and that. Even I could see I was back to my old self.

Lisa came in just as the register was being taken. Ignoring Mr Weston she came straight to me, bent towards me and whispered, 'Where were you yesterday? Got your knickers in a twist, did you?'

'Lisa!' boomed Mr Weston. She glared at him and went to her seat.

Yes, I certainly did feel different. My fear had gone, replaced by the determination to take action. Taking action felt good. It put me back in the driving seat. It diminished Lisa, and strengthened me. Yet I couldn't pretend I felt calm. I had the jitters and could feel tension contracting every muscle in my body.

Double English language was next. I walked unhurriedly to the classroom knowing Lisa was close behind me, almost feeling her breathing down my neck. She deliberately jostled me as we entered the classroom, intent on getting a reaction. She was disappointed. Miss Unsworth was already there, putting the finishing touches to some first-year work she was pinning up. I went straight up to her.

'Are we giving those talks today?'

'Yes, Jac. Have you got something for us?'

'Yeah, if that's OK.'

'Excellent.'

I sat down. A few other people had come in with talks prepared. I was pleased. That gave me time to collect myself. First off was a boy in our form who was interested in the history of trams. He spoke for a quarter of an hour, and I have to admit there was a certain amount of fidgeting but, to give Miss Unsworth credit, she looked entranced. She complimented him on the thoroughness of his research and his painstaking approach. Then Phil, another boy, had brought his guitar and played a version of 'Wonderwall'. Afterwards he spoke about Oasis. That went down very well, and Miss Unsworth said it was a first-rate talk. Phil looked as embarrassed as if he'd been asked to take his clothes off in public.

Then a girl stood up to talk about a weekend she'd had in London and after a few minutes got stage fright. Miss Unsworth told us to prompt her with questions, so we did. She relaxed after that and told us some quite interesting stuff. When she went to sit down, Miss Unsworth caught my eye. I nodded.

'Jac?' she asked. I rose. I heard Lisa's snort of contempt. I didn't mind. I took my notes with me and went to the front of the classroom.

The view was different from out there. Before, I'd sat at the front with everyone behind me and I couldn't see what they were doing. Now, they were all exposed to me. I stood; they sat. My legs were shaking, true, but no one could see them because I stood behind the teacher's desk. My shaking legs were my little secret.

'Miss Unsworth, ladies, gentlemen.' I knew everyone would laugh at the formal address, but I wanted to start like that. It made me feel as if I was acting, as if this wasn't really me. 'Like a lot of you, I've been working on the Holocaust history assignment. I was in the library, and I found this quote:

They came after the Jews. And I was not a Jew. So I did not object.

Then they came after the Catholics. And I was not a Catholic. So I did not object.

Then they came after the trade unionists. I was not a trade unionist. So I did not object.

Then they came after me. And there was no one left to object.

I like this quote because it explains why we have to do something when people are being hunted down. It also makes you feel that people should never have to suffer in silence.'

I glanced at Miss Unsworth and took a deep breath to steady my nerves.

'I'm not going to suffer in silence any more, either. But

first of all, before I explain what's been happening to me, I know I'm new here, and you don't know me very well, so I'll tell you about me. I've just turned sixteen and my hobbies are acting, chilling out with my mates, Pulp, soaps on TV and hitting the shops. My old school was Chillingham and I know a lot of you think I might be a bit posh because of it but, believe me, I'm not. I'm just like all of you. And if you still think I'm stuck-up, you should come round my place on Friday night and see what slobbing out really means.' There was some appreciative laughter. I felt encouraged.

'I can see I might seem different to you on the surface, but we're all the same underneath. I've got another quote here – it's Shakespeare – from *The Merchant of Venice*. It's spoken by Shylock, a Jew.

If you prick us, do we not bleed? If you tickle us, do we not laugh? If you poison us, do we not die?

OK, no one's tried to poison me. But in a way, that is kind of what's been going on here. There is someone in school who doesn't like me, and that's OK, I can handle that. But she is intent on making my life a misery. First it was just the odd insult, but then she put a used tampon in my school bag for me to find. Then she spread rumours about me so I wouldn't have any friends. In some ways, that was the worst bit. I reckon people need friends as much as they need food and shelter. I've read that some people who are isolated like that feel as if they can't go on living. Some kids have killed themselves because of bullying.

The girl who's been bullying me didn't stop at turning

people against me. She arranged for some lads to get me at the Lemon Tree, and now she's threatening me with violence. I've got here the note she sent me on Monday – '

I picked it up and tore it up in front of them.

'That's how much I care about it. I'm not prepared to give in to threats any longer. I haven't done anything wrong. There's nothing wrong with me the way I am. I just want you all to know what I've been going through. My life's been hell for the past few weeks. If you've been too scared yourself to speak out, actually, I understand. I was the same, in a way. But nobody should put up with bullying.

Anyway, you've heard my side of the story. It's only fair you should hear the other side, if there is another side. Since Lisa Webb, who's been bullying me, is in this group, she can have her say if she wants. I've finished.'

There wasn't a murmur. I clutched on to the edge of the teacher's desk. Lisa looked white with anger. Then, from the back of the classroom, two boys began to clap. The clapping spread. It was appreciative clapping, given to support me. I saw Claire join in enthusiastically. As she did, the other girls began to applaud. Miss Unsworth joined in, and soon everyone was clapping, and some people even cheered.

It was the best feeling I'd ever had in my life.

Everyone was clapping, except one person. She stood up, scowling, and made for the door.

'Not so fast, young lady,' Miss Unsworth said. 'I'll have the pieces of that note, Jac.' She took them and escorted Lisa out of the classroom, 'I think the head might like to have a few words with you.' Lisa tried to struggle from Miss Unsworth's grasp, but to no avail. We all watched her go.

As soon as they left, there was an explosion of chatter. Claire left her place and came over to me.

'You were great, Jac. I'm so pleased you said all that.'

I smiled weakly. All I wanted to do now was sit down. Some lads came up to me.

'Can we come round to your place on Friday night,' they asked, 'and see you slobbing out?'

'Push off,' I said.

'No – we're serious, honest. We live round your way. We can go on to the pub after.'

Another girl came over. 'That was a dead good speech. You ought to go into politics. None of us really liked her. Did you know a kid in the first year left on account of her? Lisa's a cow.'

'It was right what you said in your talk,' someone else said. 'We were all scared of her. I'm sorry if I've not said anything. I thought what she did to you last Friday was terrible.'

And there were more comments like that. Claire and some other girls moved my stuff over to their seats, and I went to join them. I was accepted now, and it felt peculiar. I wasn't used to it yet. I couldn't help but wonder what was happening to Lisa. I felt no desire for revenge, just a wish never to see her again.

In fact, I never did. I noticed Leanne and Jodie weren't at afternoon registration either, and Claire was called away from lessons for a bit. Leanne and Jodie apologised to me, and I said it was OK. Deep down, of course, it wasn't. If I was a better person I might have been able to forgive them, but I'm only me. Then rumours began to circulate about Lisa. Some people said she'd been expelled and others that she'd only been suspended but she refused to come back to school after. I wasn't bothered to find out the exact truth. It was enough that she had gone, and I could start picking up my life again.

I walked down my road that afternoon, happy but exhausted, and only then remembered my mother's interview. I hoped it had gone well for her. I let myself in and she was in the kitchen, chopping vegetables for dinner.

'How did it go?' I asked.

'Oh, OK. But they're keeping us on tenterhooks. We won't find out the results till tomorrow. At least, that's what I was told. But the interview wasn't too bad.' And she launched into a blow-by-blow account of it.

I let her go on until she'd finished. I knew she'd have an awful night worrying about the result, so I thought I was duty-bound to distract her. We each took a drink into the living-room and sat down.

'Mum,' I said. 'I've had a kind of interesting day, too. But I'm going to have to go right back to the beginning to explain.'

Seventeen

I was still a bit of a celebrity on Friday, and was even invited into the head's office with Miss Unsworth for a congratulatory chat. That was something I could have done without. Heads always scare the hell out of me, the way they sit behind huge desks and get up to shake your hand like you're at some sort of high-powered meeting.

Also I was keen for the whole business to settle down now. I suppose I felt a bit like someone who'd had an operation and just needed a bit of rest and space to recover. As the day went on and things began to go back to normal, I started to pick up the pieces of my old life. I saw Neil again in the corridor; he smiled but said nothing. I realised then that Rachel hadn't rung me all week. I had a pretty good idea why. I wondered whether I was strong enough yet to ring her and congratulate her on hooking Neil. We'd see.

When I got home that evening I thought it would be as well to ring her as soon as possible to get it over with. As much as I was smitten with Neil, Rachel meant far more to me. Had it not been for Rachel I wouldn't have survived the past few weeks. I owed her everything. I owed her Neil.

I went into the hall to call her when I heard someone at the door. My mother? I wondered whether she'd had the result of her interview. In fact, it was both my parents. They looked quite happy – had they been out celebrating?

'Did you get the job?' I asked.

'No,' my mother said. 'No. And they told me my services wouldn't be required next year.'

'Oh, no!' This was bad news. Only I didn't understand why she didn't look upset. In fact she looked years younger.

'Come on. We can't all stand here in the hall,' Dad said. 'Into the living-room. Come on, Jac. Move yourself.'

We all went into the living-room and I hastily began to tidy away my mess.

'You needn't do that now,' Mum said.

Then I knew something must be up.

'Yes, the principal called me in this morning to explain they wouldn't be needing me. And do you know, something snapped. I thought, they've treated me like rubbish for years. I actually felt quite angry. And I realised that it wasn't too late for me to give in my notice for Easter. So I did. I told them I wouldn't be requiring their job.'

'Mum!'

'And I felt so relieved. I've never got on with Valerie, and listening to you yesterday, I realised in her own way she was a bully, too. So I'm free. And I rang Dad at the warehouse, and we went out for lunch – '

So that was why she was looking flushed.

'– and for some time Dad's been talking about employing someone to look after the office side of things, and we realised I could work for him. It simplifies everything. It's a risk, but there are times when you have to take a risk.'

Dad kissed her then. I wished he wouldn't do that kind of thing in public. I mean, they're *parents*, for heaven's sake. I congratulated Mum, while Dad went to the cabinet for his favourite whisky and some sherry. He looked enquiringly at me.

'I've got a phone call to make first,' I said.

I really had to ring Rachel. I didn't feel I could leave it another minute. There was so much to say to her. Perhaps I could get the bus round to her place tonight. We had a lot of catching up to do.

As I approached the phone, it rang. This often happens. Rach and I are so close that frequently we think of ringing each other at the same time. I lifted the receiver.

'Hi, Rach?'

'Jac?'

That wasn't Rachel's voice. It was a male voice. A familiar male voice.

'Yeah?'

'It's Neil.'

'I know.' Brilliant conversationalist, aren't I?

'Hey, I heard what happened to you – you know, about Lisa Webb. I didn't know any of that was going on. If I did, I'd have killed her. I didn't find out till this afternoon. You gave a speech in English, didn't you?'

'Yeah.' Little Miss Eloquent, I was.

'That was really cool. Well done. But I'm really sorry you had to go through that. You hid it well in rehearsals.'

'Thanks.' I just couldn't think of anything to say to him.

'Hey, listen. I was going to ring you anyway.'

Now something occurred to me. 'But I never gave you my number.'

'Yeah, I know. I got it off Rachel.'

'Rachel?'

'Yeah. Look, do you fancy going bowling on Saturday?'

'What? With you and Rachel?'

'Me, Rachel and Mike. You know, Mike fancies Rachel.'

'He does?'

'Don't sound so surprised!'

'No, that's great. She likes him, too.'

'Great.'

A horrible, embarrassing silence.

'Well, are you coming out with us?'

'Yeah,' I said. 'I might.'

'Fantastic. I'll meet you there at eight.'

'Yeah. See ya.' Slowly I replaced the receiver, hardly daring to believe what had happened. After a moment or two to collect myself, I dialled Rachel's number.

'Rach?'

'Jac?'

'You know who's just rung me?'

'Might do.'

'You scheming little – '

'No – listen. He rang me in the week. He just wanted to know if you were interested in him. Then I didn't want to tell you he'd rung in case it got your hopes up. Is this cool or what? But first of all, how's school?'

'How long have you got?'

'As long as it takes.'

'Well, get a load of this . . .'

For the last time I looked in the mirror at the Lemon Tree. As adult as I was now, I knew I would always carry inside me the vulnerability and pain of the girl who'd been bullied, but also the knowledge that it was possible to fight back.

I brushed my hair again. For the rest of my time at Markfield I'd been reasonably happy. I did well at my GCSEs, then went on to sixth-form college to study English literature, history and theatre studies. My A Levels had gone according to plan, and I got the grades I'd needed for uni.

Rachel stayed on at Chillingham, but together we started a youth branch of Amnesty, the human-rights pressure group, with members from both my college and her school. The group's still going strong. As is her relationship with Mike. If ever a match was made in heaven . . .

I don't know what became of Lisa. I wish I could say that she reformed, or that in some way she got what she deserved. I don't feel sorry for her. I know there's a lot of talk these days about having to understand why bullies do the things they do, and there is something in that, but it's not an excuse. Not everyone who is abused or badly treated as a child turns into a criminal. And nothing excuses cruelty. That's what I think, anyway.

Lisa left school before her GCSEs. I don't know if she took them elsewhere. Claire told me she'd left home, moved out of town, shacked up with some bloke, and was looking more glamorous than ever. More importantly, Markfield instituted an anti-bullying code, our class took an assembly on it and later the school set up a bullying court. There was a feature about it in the local paper.

In case you're wondering, I did go out with Neil for a while. It lasted until the end of our first term at sixth-form college. Then we just agreed to be friends and see other people. In fact, Neil should have been here tonight, but he's away in France with his parents. I had a postcard from him yesterday. Funnily enough, we're going to the same uni. At least I'll know one person there. Facing the future alone can be scary.

But enough of the future. The present is sufficient right now. I have one last night with my best mates, and I'm not going to stand here thinking any longer. I'm going back out there, and I'll be making sure it's a night we'll never forget!

Resources

If you think you're being bullied, don't suffer in silence. Tell yourself it's not your fault – it's the bully's fault.

Then take action. Remember, you don't have to deal with this problem alone. Talk to someone. If you're being bullied at school, talk to a teacher. Pick the one you get on with best, so you're comfortable and don't feel tempted to make light of your suffering. If the bullying takes place out of school, talk to a responsible adult, a parent, or an older member of your family. Talk to your friends, too. Nobody likes bullies, and the chances are your friends will be on your side.

If you feel there's no one you can talk to, you can call or write to the following organisations and they will give you all the support and help you need – and it's all confidential.

Anti-Bullying Campaign
Tel: 0171 378 1446

Childline
Tel: 0800 1111 – calls are free, are answered round the clock and won't show up on your parents' bill.

Kidscape
2 Grosvenor Gardens
London SWIW 0DH
Tel: 0171 730 3300 during office hours – they will send you booklets on how to beat bullying.

National Society for the Prevention of Cruelty to Children
Tel: 0800 800 500 – calls are free and the line is open 24 hours a day.

Samaritans
Tel: 0345 909090 – you can ring any time, or even drop in to one of their centres.

Most of all – speak out!